*"Which night?" Corrie heard herself asking.*

She'd never been a coward, but having Nick over for supper would perhaps be the greatest act of courage in her life.

"If not tomorrow night," Nick said, "then the next night. Or the next." He gave her a smile that slanted a little. "It's rude to invite myself, but I hope you'll overlook the bad manners."

Now his smile widened and her heart fluttered wildly. "My, my, Corrie. You look like you think I might be up to no good."

"Are you?" she dared softly. "Up to no good?"

"If I am, I'm confident you'll set me straight."

**Susan Fox** lives in Des Moines, Iowa. A lifelong fan of Westerns, cowboys and love stories with guaranteed happy endings, she tends to think of romantic heroes in terms of Stetsons and boots.

Fans may visit her Web site at www.susanfox.org

## Books by Susan Fox

Don't miss any of our special offers. Write to us at the following address for information on our newest releases.

Harlequin Reader Service
U.S.: 3010 Walden Ave., P.O. Box 1325, Buffalo, NY 14269
Canadian: P.O. Box 609, Fort Erie, Ont. L2A 5X3

# THE BRIDE PRIZE

## Susan Fox

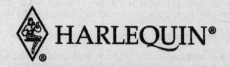

TORONTO • NEW YORK • LONDON
AMSTERDAM • PARIS • SYDNEY • HAMBURG
STOCKHOLM • ATHENS • TOKYO • MILAN • MADRID
PRAGUE • WARSAW • BUDAPEST • AUCKLAND

ISBN 0-373-03828-3

THE BRIDE PRIZE

First North American Publication 2005.

Copyright © 2004 by Susan Fox.

www.eHarlequin.com

**Printed in U.S.A.**

# CHAPTER ONE

THE land was brutal and big, and her small ranch sat like a postage stamp in the vastness. The work was hard, the hours long. Dirt and sweat and sometimes blood made for a less than aesthetic or antiseptic environment. It wasn't a safe environment either. The animals were large and even the best-behaved and best-trained could be dangerous on a bad day. Accidents happened, both to the unwary and to the vigilant. Things fouled up and broke down. Trouble could blow in from the west in a fierce storm or slither from beneath a rock.

Not the place for a lady, but Corrie Davis had given up on being a lady. There'd been a brief time at eighteen when she'd tried to rise above her plain-Jane, mostly tomboy life; a time when she'd gone out of her way to adapt to things like panty hose and makeup. She'd devoured books on etiquette from the local library, bought more than a few women's magazines, and she'd spent a whole weekend in San Antonio to buy some extra dressy, extra feminine things.

Things which now hung, with tags still attached, in her closet, while the frilly unmentionables from that modest shopping spree languished in a drawer, unworn.

The man who'd inspired her brief rush toward femininity had unknowingly crushed the impulse with a few solemn words.

*You're bright, Corrie, and you're sensible. I reckon you've figured out by now that you aren't the girl for my brother. Our daddy has plans for Shane, plans for college, plans for him to take on his share of Merrick business. These next months and years, he'll be testing his limits, finding his place...*

Nick Merrick had paused then and given her a level look, his dark gaze impacting hers in a way that had made her heart pound with dread and shame, because she'd already sensed what he'd say next.

*You won't fit into that, Corrie. I'd hate to see you break your heart trying.*

Much as hearing Nick Merrick say those things had hurt, he'd been right. She wouldn't have fit into his father's plans for his younger brother's life. And she certainly wasn't the woman Shane Merrick should marry. But that was because she'd had no wish to fit into Shane's life and even fewer intentions of marrying him. Not then, not ever.

Corrie would ever be grateful that Nick had never figured out the truth: that *he'd* been the man she'd been in love with back then, not Shane. It had been Nick she'd hoped to attract with those pretty dresses and prissy manners. Letting her know so straightforwardly that he considered her unsuitable for his brother had seemed to confirm Nick's personal opinion of her. He might as well have been speaking about himself.

And of course, since she'd hardly been the kind of girl men flocked around or tried to date anyway—and still wasn't—what he'd said seemed to also confirm the dismal knowledge that she might never appeal to a man other than as a friend. In fact it had been her "just one of the boys" appeal that had won Shane's friendship in the first place.

It still amazed her that Nick Merrick had thought there'd been anything more than friendship involved, but the idea that he'd thought either she or Shane had been contemplating marriage had been a shock.

Corrie hadn't recalled that embarrassing conversation for years now. Once she'd got past the hurt, she'd pushed it all behind her and managed to go on as if nothing had happened. Her father had passed away shortly before she'd turned twenty, so she'd had more than enough to fill her days and crowd out any lingering interest in either of the Merrick brothers.

Aside from the fact that Merrick Ranch bordered hers, there hadn't been much cause for social contact, so she'd rarely had to deal with Nick again. Shane had gone off to college, as planned, but he'd left after the first semester to pursue his rodeo dream. So much for the life Nick and their late father had mapped out for him.

In truth, Corrie had heard from Shane so infrequently in the past six years that she hardly ever thought about him anymore. Until yesterday when Nick had left a message on her answering machine. Since then, her memories of that time had come drifting back.

Nick had obviously taken for granted that she'd had contact with his brother. *When you see Shane, would you have him give me a call?*

The out-of-the-blue message had taken her completely by surprise. She hadn't planned to call Nick back because the message had led her to believe she'd soon see Shane and would be able to pass on the request.

Now it had been over twenty-four hours and there'd been no sign of him. Surely Nick had heard from Shane himself by now, so there was still no reason to phone him unless he'd left a second message asking her to.

The walk from the stable to the house seemed particularly long after the tiring morning she'd put in. She was a hot, filthy mess, with grease stains on her hands and beneath her short fingernails, probably some in her hair, a torn sleeve and a layer of dust over the rest of her. Visual proof of a frustrating tinker with a windmill and a bruising fall from the colt she'd been working. Both had been extra chores she wished now she'd put off until she'd been less distracted.

After a quick shower and change of clothes, she'd get a cold lunch then make a pass at paperwork and take care of a few things around the house. Safe enough pursuits while she tried again to banish the

Merrick brothers from her mind and put the past back in the past, where it belonged.

As she walked along, she was inspecting the torn shirtsleeve and debating whether to sew it or cut it off, when a laughing male voice drew her gaze to the back porch.

"What's the other guy look like?"

Shane Merrick was sitting on the porch rail, handsome as ever, dressed in an outlaw black Stetson and a jewel blue, pearl snap Western shirt that matched his eyes. His jeans still carried enough color to look reasonably new, and his black boots had a subtle, go-to-town shine, but it was the large gold belt buckle that proclaimed his champion rodeo status that completed the picture.

As she took the two steps up onto the porch, Shane eased off the rail and came toward her. The instant she realized he was about to sweep her into a hug, Corrie put up a hand and took a hasty step away.

"You'll get dirty."

"A little dirt won't hurt." In that next moment, he caught her against him in a tight hug, startling a self-conscious laugh from her. "Damn, but it's good to see you, Corrie."

The words were wonderful to hear and the hug far too personal, but she was careful not to take them as anything more than they were.

"You're looking good too, stranger. And you smell downright pretty." She drew back and grinned up at him as she righted her Stetson. "How's the champion bronc rider? Going for a third buckle?"

Shane smiled down at her and lifted a hand to pluck a wayward lock of dark hair off her cheek that had worked out of her braid. "Took me long enough to get that far. Might as well quit while I'm ahead."

As Corrie pulled farther away, she reached for the door. "How about something cold to drink?"

"Sounds good."

She led the way into the house and hung her Stetson on a wall peg before she walked to the sink.

"Help yourself to whatever you want. I need to get at least one layer of dirt off."

She rolled up one shirtsleeve then did what she could with what was left of the other before she turned on the faucet and reached for the bar of soap and small hand brush in the dish next to the sink. In seconds, she'd worked up a lather then set about scouring the grease stains from her hands and from beneath her nails.

"Name your poison," Shane called and she glanced over to where he stood in front of the open refrigerator door.

"Ice water for me," she said, then turned back to her task.

She heard him close the refrigerator then walk to her side to hold the glass of water within reach. She turned her head a little to smile at him.

"Thanks. Just set it down till I get a little cleaner."

"You look good enough to me."

Corrie had been about to look away when he'd said that, but she detected a flash of something new in his blue eyes, something that flustered her. She pulled her gaze away to give her fingernails another going over with the small brush. After a quick rinse she soaped up again and bent over the sink to wash her face before she rinsed and blindly turned off the tap.

She put out a wet hand for the towel, but Shane pushed it into her fingers. Once she'd dried her face, she took care of her hands.

"Your brother left a message yesterday. Wanted you to call." She finished with the towel and tossed it aside to reach for the glass as she added, "But I reckon you've had time to get home by now though."

"Been home, heard the pitch."

Corrie picked up the glass and had a reviving drink before she turned and briefly leaned back against the counter. Shane still had the pitcher, so she held out her glass for a refill.

"The pitch?" she asked after he'd finished pouring.

Shane walked to the refrigerator to put the pitcher away. "He's willing to let me rule and reign with him without a business or agricultural degree."

Corrie studied his face when he turned back to her and saw that his earlier teasing smile had flattened. "It's a good offer, isn't it?"

Shane made an attempt at a half smile. "I don't think I'm cut out for that fifty-five/forty-five split. Aside from the fact that Nick has more say, there's

also the fact that I haven't contributed forty-five percent, so I don't reckon I deserve equal control. Less
trouble to buy a place of my own, be my own boss.''

Corrie didn't comment on that, but she wasn't surprised. Shane had a strong independent streak. Proof
of that had been his frequent clashes with his father
and older brother, then after old Jake's death and just
before he'd started college, Shane's clashes with Nick
had multiplied. The fact that Shane had left school to
pursue his own plans had been the ultimate declaration.

She didn't agree that Shane wasn't entitled to his
inheritance though. Being born to a Merrick entitled
him just as being born to a Davis had entitled her to
her inheritance.

"Let's go in and sit down," she said, then led the
way out of the kitchen into the hall. She heard Shane
chuckle softly.

"Might be a good time to mention that there's a
hand-size grease spot on the right cheek of your
britches.''

Corrie halted to glance back to see if he was teasing
or serious, and of course, his blue gaze danced with
amusement.

"Truly?"

Instead of answering, Shane held up the folded
newspaper he must have picked up off the kitchen
table on his way past. "You can sit on this.''

Corrie walked on into the living room. She waited
while he opened the newspaper on the seat of an over-

stuffed chair before she dropped down on the cushion, grateful for the soft landing, and that she'd managed not to spill her glass of ice water.

Shane took a seat on the upholstered footstool that matched the old chair. He nodded toward her glass.

"By rights, that water should have slopped all over. You always did have a kind of elegance."

Again Corrie caught a glimpse of...something...in his gaze. And again she tried to ignore it and made a doubtful face.

"No more elegance than the nearest gate half off its hinges."

A little of his smile faded. "You still don't know how to take a compliment. You probably haven't figured out yet that most of the men in these parts make eyes at you and think naughty thoughts."

The shock of hearing him say that was second only to the flash of shame she felt. Men barely noticed her, and it stung a little to have him call attention to it, even in a backhanded way.

She smiled as if it didn't matter, blew out a half-embarrassed, half-exasperated breath, then reached back to catch her braid and bring it over her shoulder to strip the leather tie from the end. Braided, her dark hair went to just below her shoulder blades. Unbound, her hair fell nearly to her waist.

"Maybe I ought to send you to the barn for a shovel before it gets too deep in here," she told him as she set the glass of water aside to start unraveling her braid.

And immediately wished she hadn't when she caught sight of the solemn expression that dropped over Shane's tanned face as he watched her fingers work. That odd, fluttery feeling came winging back and she immediately tried to suppress it.

"I don't mean to be rude and bossy," she said then, "but would you mind picking another place to sit so I can pry off these boots? The seam on my sock hasn't set right all day."

Shane dealt her another small surprise when instead of obliging, he grinned and reached down for her right boot to lift her foot. The gesture was completely new between them, and she was too caught off guard to do anything but stare as he pulled off her boot and set it down.

"I interrupted a stampede to the shower didn't I?" One side of his handsome mouth quirked up.

Corrie was still a little too surprised to realize until after he'd leaned down to reach for her other foot that his arm had effectively trapped her ankle on top of his hard thigh.

"You never minded getting dirty," he remarked, "but once you got to the house you were always in a girlish rush to get cleaned up."

Then he had her other foot up and was stripping off the boot before he settled that foot next to the other on his thigh. The idea of having both her feet in his lap seemed incredibly intimate, which finally goaded her out of her silence.

"Is there a reason you're so friendly with my

feet?'' she asked as she pulled them back, relieved when he allowed it.

"No good reason," he admitted. "Just wondered how long you'd let me do it. You ever had a foot massage?"

"Nope. Don't want one either." Corrie felt a little prudish suddenly for taking this so seriously, but something had changed between them. Shane had always treated her as a pal, one of the guys. He was gentler with her of course, but there'd never been even a hint of real man/woman things, or even much acknowledgment that she was female.

Yes, there'd been that time when she'd turned her head at the wrong time as he'd been leaning over to whisper something silly to her. His lips had brushed hers, but they'd both jumped back as if they'd been burned. Then they'd laughed like hyenas over it. This wasn't at all like that one time.

Now Shane's smile leveled a little, but the intent look—that *new* look—in his eyes sent heat into her face. "You're still an innocent, aren't you, Corrie?" His voice dropped lower. "I can't tell you how rare and special that is out there in that big, wide world."

Corrie gave him a wary look, unsure what to say to that. Or to any of this. That seemed to tickle him. His face brightened and he chuckled as he leaned forward to tug on a lock of her hair before he abruptly stood.

"You go get that shower, darlin'. I need to get on down the road, but I'll call you later. 'Kay?"

*Darlin'?* Corrie's gaze was all but glued to his and she'd been unable to break contact with it as he'd risen. Her soft and belated, "'Kay," was part squeak, part whisper, as if she'd somehow lost her voice.

She didn't get up as she watched him turn and stride to the hall then to the front door. Once he was out of sight, her gaze fell and fixed on the footstool.

Confusion swamped her, and for the first time in her life, Corrie felt the magnitude of her inexperience. She could talk work or business or politics with just about any man, but she was ignorant about male/female things. She knew about courting and the mechanics of sex, but she had only hazy theories about how those things actually got started in real life.

Or, more specifically, in *her* life. The boys she'd grown up around hadn't minded working alongside her on roundup or doing ranch work or on projects at school. She was a hard worker and they'd liked that she'd pulled her own weight and that she wasn't squeamish or timid with the stock. And she'd been a favorite in classroom situations where the teacher wanted boys and girls to work together. Probably because she'd gotten good grades in everything, and the boys hadn't needed to worry that Corrie Davis would get lovestruck and moon over one of them.

But when it had come to school dances and other dating opportunities, they'd passed her up like a mailbox along a highway. Town girls and girls who'd learned how to bat their eyelashes and flirt had gotten the dates. Girls who'd worn makeup and panty hose and short little blouses and skirts that bared midriffs and thighs. Girls who'd seemed to have been born knowing how to use their female powers to wrap boyfriends around their little fingers. Not girls like her, who could rope and ride, arm-wrestle them on a dare, bait a fishhook, and go hunting.

It had been the town girls' example that she'd tried to follow when she'd fallen for Nick Merrick. Some of those girls had been plain, but they'd made over their plainness with eye shadow and other little beauty tricks from magazines. Her mistake had been in thinking Corrie Davis could do the same, with the same happy results.

Thinking of all that again reminded her that she'd been feeling more than a little weary of the sameness of her life lately, the solitude. She'd been in town from time to time the past few weeks, and seen a handful of old schoolmates with their husbands and kids. She'd told herself that being twenty-four wasn't anywhere near old maid status, not at all. But she'd felt a little low for a while.

Now Shane Merrick was home and he was… flirting with her? The fact that she'd never had a man flirt with her made her uncertain, though the rare, so rare thrill of the notion excited her.

Corrie propped an elbow on the chair arm, not realizing for several moments that she'd pressed her fingers against her mouth.

Had Shane been flirting?

The numbing sameness of her life had lifted the

past few minutes. It'd probably be back again tomorrow, but today...

Today the pattern—the rut—had been broken. That low feeling was gone, though she wasn't sure she trusted the reason. She wasn't even sure the reason was real, and yet suddenly she had the feeling that for the first time in her plain-Jane, tomboy life, she might actually have a chance for a little romance.

To maybe fall in love a little with a man who might fall a little in love with her. Maybe she wasn't so impossible after all. Maybe love wasn't so impossible. And if love was possible for Corrie Davis, maybe marriage and kids were also possible. Maybe. At some point.

By the time she got her shower, ate lunch and tried to concentrate on paperwork, she was struggling between common sense and the tantalizing notion of possibility. Common sense finally won out, as it always did, and that fine, all too hopeful—and a little giddy—feeling leaked away.

# CHAPTER TWO

IT WAS hard for Nick Merrick to think of Corrie Davis as a femme fatale. He still didn't understand what his kid brother had seen in her years ago, not when he compared Corrie to the pretty and far more sophisticated girls Shane had preferred in high school.

And still preferred, judging by the bevy of buckle bunnies who'd trailed him on the rodeo circuit. Two of those women had already called the ranch and left messages for him. A third had called after Shane had gone over to the Davis Ranch.

Nick assumed that's where Shane had gone, because he'd spiffed up just enough to hint he wanted to make an impression. Most of his other old girlfriends had either married or moved away, so it made sense he'd been on his way to see Corrie. Besides, five minutes after he'd walked in yesterday afternoon, he'd mentioned her. He hadn't mentioned any of the others.

Corrie Davis was the one who'd encouraged him years ago. Nick didn't know how influential she'd been over Shane during his rodeo years, but her potential to sidetrack his brother again was worth considering.

She'd grown up on a small ranch, taken it over after

her father's death and managed to keep it going. But she'd have no idea of the complexities and demands of the massive operation Merrick Ranch was, and even less about other Merrick interests.

Shane was rebel enough to still be infatuated with the idea of striking out on his own again, which was why he was bucking the notion of coming back to Merrick Ranch to stay. And of course the fact that Corrie was her own boss would also appeal to Shane. Her example as a reasonably successful small-time rancher would no doubt fuel Shane's notions of independence in a way that being handed almost half a small empire would not.

In truth Nick knew if his situation and Shane's were reversed, he too might have chafed at the notion of being a second-fiddle owner to an older brother who had final say. Nick himself might have been lured by the notion of finding a way apart from Merrick money to make his mark.

But Nick was obliged to their father and generations of Merrick history and tradition to make an effort to bring his brother back into the fold. Family duty wasn't a take it or leave it proposition, and it was past time for Shane to live up to his share of their obligation.

Their daddy had seen Shane's dream of rodeo glory as a character failing. While Nick had never agreed with that, he'd also felt the pressure of wanting his kid brother to measure up to their daddy's expectations and prove himself to their old man. Nick still wanted to see that, even if their father was no longer around.

Though he didn't like to face the idea, Nick sometimes felt as if Shane's refusal to take on his share was an indication that he'd failed to instill the right values in Shane. After all, Shane had been more his responsibility than their daddy's those last years.

Nick already knew that this was his last opportunity to persuade Shane to come home to stay. And if that meant chasing Corrie Davis away again, then it was something he was compelled to do. He'd done it before and she'd been bright enough to comply. Though Shane had gone off the track anyway, at least he hadn't married her.

On the other hand, Shane's head had been full of rodeo six years ago and maybe Corrie was sensible enough to know she wouldn't have liked driving all over the country living out of motel rooms.

And because her elderly father's health had been starting to decline, she probably wouldn't have been comfortable going off with a husband who had rodeo fever. But now that Shane was through with rodeo, the problem Corrie Davis posed had again become an issue.

Wondering what Corrie might still feel for his brother was second only to the question of why his brother was so attracted to a female like her. If he could figure that out, he might be able to find a way to make her look less attractive. And without her influence, Shane might come back into line that much sooner.

Nick was still thinking about Corrie when he heard Shane come in from the back patio and call out to their housekeeper. The fact that he was home made Nick consider the wisdom of going directly over to the Davis Ranch. If he could do something to dissuade Corrie from taking up with Shane again, it'd be better to do it right away before anything got much of a start.

He closed the computer program he'd been using and shut down, then reached for a cell phone before he headed for the kitchen. Shane was gone by the time he got there, so he let himself out the back and walked purposely toward his truck.

It took twenty minutes to drive to the Davis Ranch. Time enough to think about what he'd say, but also time enough to realize how dictatorial he'd sound. Though Corrie Davis wasn't known for a quick temper, she had more than her share of pride.

And she'd run her own small place for a little over four years. She wouldn't look favorably on a ranching neighbor she rarely saw who suddenly showed up to stick his nose into what she'd surely see as her private business.

The things she'd let him get away with saying, unchallenged, six years ago might go over badly this time. He wasn't normally a subtle man, mostly because he was too blunt and focused on efficiency to bother with subtleties. But perhaps subtlety was the only way to handle her this time.

Maybe showing up on Corrie's doorstep would be enough to remind her he was still around, still paying attention, and she'd be prompted to recall how strongly he'd once disapproved of any wedding plans between her and his brother. Maybe she'd sense that he disapproved just as strongly now. If she didn't, he could be more direct.

The drive from the highway to the Davis ranch house was little more than a mile. As he came over the slight rise that managed to block the view of the midsize house and outbuildings from the highway, his gaze homed in on the slim woman who was bent slightly over the flower beds along the east side of the house.

He recognized Corrie right away, but what got his attention was that her normally braided hair hung loose like a glossy mantle, and it now dangled like a dark curtain over the blossoms. She straightened briefly to swing that glorious length behind her back, then bent again to empty a metal pail of water near the base of the flowers.

She finished and turned to look in his direction about the time he pulled his pickup to a halt in the drive. If she was surprised to see him, she didn't show it. Of course, she had to have heard the truck engine as he'd driven closer. Plenty of time to conceal her reaction.

As he got out and started across the grass that was

more brown than green, Nick wasn't able to keep from ogling Corrie's beautiful hair. But that only lasted a second or so before his gaze moved over the rest of her.

He didn't see Corrie often, and usually only at a distance. Seeing her now, dressed in an old white T-shirt that had shrunk enough to cling a little, and cut-off jeans that ended high enough to show most of the length of her sleekly muscled legs, was very nearly a shock. And she was barefoot. She'd been dressed for ranch work almost every time he'd ever seen her, so to see her like this with a good half mile of leg showing, hit him like a two-by-four across the chest.

*Hadn't Shane just come from here?* Was *he* the reason her hair was down and looked fresh-washed, and she was dressed in a way that, on her, was decidedly provocative compared to her usual wholesome appearance? And yet, she still looked wholesome. Wholesome, but appealing as all get out.

Corrie hadn't thought Nick Merrick would show up, much less this soon, so she steeled herself. And wished to heaven she'd dressed in something more appropriate for company than a T-shirt and cutoffs after her shower. Since it was late enough in the afternoon, she'd thought it was a good time to water her flowers before she forgot, never dreaming someone would see her.

As she watched Nick Merrick stride toward her, she

saw the bold sweep of his male gaze go over her, and
she tried to look unaffected. Trying to appear unaffected by Nick Merrick's nearness was a pretense
she'd mastered long ago, but no man—much less
Nick—had ever had an opportunity to see her bare
legs, so it was a little harder to appear indifferent this
time.

Desperate to distract herself from the way his gaze
felt as it skimmed then lingered then skimmed again,
she began to catalog the similarities and contrasts between the brothers.

Shane was the more handsome of the two, though
they both had similar features and coloring. The difference between the brothers was amplified by the
eight years that separated them. Shane's handsomeness was smoother and a little boyish, but Nick's had
been seasoned by sun and weather and experience
into a rugged toughness that made him look hard and
forbidding. And worlds more compelling.

His black hair and black brows emphasized the
piercing blackness of his gaze, while Shane's eyes
were an electric blue. Both men were the same six
foot plus height, but Nick was more heavily muscled,
despite Shane's competitive fitness as a world champion bronc rider.

And Nick didn't have the cowboy swagger Shane
often showed, as if he was too purposeful and sure of
himself to move in the cocky way some men did
when they had something to prove.

Maybe that was because Nick had proved himself

long ago, after his father had been crippled by a riding accident and confined to a wheelchair. Nick had left college to take over Merrick Ranch and take up the reins to everything else until he'd delegated enough to managers to concentrate most of his day-to-day energies on the massive chunk of Texas the Merricks owned.

The result was this harsh-looking, rawhide tough, formidable man, who wore authority as if he'd been born with it. He certainly had been born *to* it, and Corrie doubted he'd ever had a chance to be a lesser man. Not because a man like him would ever leave himself without a choice, but because it wasn't in his nature to be less than he was.

He was a man who gave his best and expected the best in return. The woman he picked to marry would also be the best. She'd be beautiful and sophisticated and rich, with a pedigree as impressive as his.

Which had shut Corrie out of consideration at eighteen, and still did. A female like her had about as much chance of attracting a man like Nick Merrick as she had of jumping off the barn roof and flying to San Antonio.

That unhappy reality had no impact whatsoever on the odd, inner twang she'd felt every time Nick had ever come in close range. As he crossed those few remaining feet between them, the twang began to quiver and hum. When he halted in front of her and lifted his hand to briefly pinch the brim of his hat in a cowboy signal of politeness, she felt a dismaying heat go over her from head to toe...

Wary blue eyes, with feathery black lashes that any number of his old girlfriends would have killed to have, had watched him, searching his face as he'd walked closer, dropping to his shoulders then his chest before they'd shot back up, as if she didn't want to be caught looking him over like women usually did. Nick couldn't help liking that. Corrie Davis had never seemed to have a sexually forward or flirty bone in her body, and she apparently still didn't.

But now that he was looking at her this close, he wondered why he'd ever thought her face was unremarkable. Her blue eyes had always been her best feature, but now the rest of her face had caught up. She had fine, lightly tanned skin, facial features that had evened out and matured into simple beauty, and a mouth that looked soft and vulnerable and intriguing.

Whatever his brother had seen in Corrie before had obviously blossomed, and Nick suddenly realized he might be in the fight of his life if he tried to come between Shane and this...lovely young woman. Was every man in this part of Texas as blind as he'd been?

He was surprised to hear the gravely burr in his voice as he nodded to her and said, "Miss Davis."

She nodded back but didn't speak right away. In that little pulse of time she managed to blank the wariness from her gaze. "If you're looking for Shane, he left quite a while ago. Maybe three hours."

"I'll catch up with him later then." Belatedly, he realized he ought to compliment her on the flowers. But when he looked at them to make the compliment credible, her bare legs came into sharp focus again and the only compliments he could think of for a second or two were a half dozen variations that included the words "long stems."

"You've got some beautiful flowers, Ms. Davis." He lifted his gaze—a surprisingly difficult task—to her face.

He'd hesitated slightly before he'd said the word *flowers* to convey his other meaning. The color that surged into her cheeks told him she'd caught it.

He smiled, satisfied by that, and nodded toward the metal pail. "Can I give you a hand?"

Nick would have offered to do the same for any female, but he'd be willing to bet money that most men wouldn't have asked the very capable and self-sufficient Corrie Davis. But women were women, and he sensed she was pleased with the offer. He sensed just as strongly that she'd decline.

"Thanks, but that was the last of it."

He could tell she felt awkward with the silence that came next, but he waited her out. Better to keep her a little on edge so she'd get the idea that he wasn't someone she wanted to tangle with.

And yet during that scattering of seconds as he looked over at her, something shifted in his attitude.

His brother could do worse than Corrie Davis, far worse. What was actually wrong with the woman herself? She was decent, hardworking, and honest.

As he allowed those first inklings of change, he tried to tell himself that it had nothing to do with seeing Corrie like this. It took a few moments more to make himself remember what he'd come here for. And why.

Corrie Davis might be decent and hardworking and honest, but she had the potential to sidetrack his brother again. Maybe more than ever now that he'd got a close up look at exactly what she had to offer.

If Shane married her, the idea of perhaps combining her little ranch with his plan to buy the ranch for sale down the road, might fuel Shane's latest bull-headed bid for independence. And Nick knew for a fact that another small ranch would soon be coming onto the market, and Shane might also want to snap it up. His kid brother had managed to put together enough winnings in the past three years to be able to strap himself to a hell of a mortgage.

It's what he'd do if he were Shane's age and he hadn't already become permanently addicted to the even riskier challenge of running Merrick Ranch. If his brother had his kind of drive, then starting from scratch under his own power with his own earnings would be an irresistible challenge that would more than prove his Merrick heritage.

That challenge would test everything Shane had ever learned about ranching, and put his mind and body and will to the test of a lifetime. A woman like Corrie Davis would share the work and the worry. And, from the look of her now, provide a hefty share of the reward.

The idea that suddenly came to him then was about strategy, though he had to admit that it had been inspired by the feminine loveliness he was staring at.

Was it possible to make Corrie an ally?

First he'd have to find out exactly what was between her and his brother. And since the quickest way to find out was to put the two of them together in the same room so he could see it for himself, Nick decided he might as well arrange it now. He gave a slight smile to banish some of the tension he'd hoped to build in her. He regretted doing that now.

"I was thinking it might be a nice surprise for Shane if I asked you to supper tonight. I know it's short notice, so we could do it tomorrow if you'd rather. I'm not much for dressing up after the day I put in, so I'm hoping you wouldn't mind if we kept things casual tonight. Maybe we could save something more formal for another time."

It was amazing how easily the lie rolled off his tongue. He'd spent the day indoors doing paperwork. But the goal was to make Corrie feel comfortable coming to the ranch. Folks tended to be overawed, and Corrie was about as country as they came. He knew for a fact that she'd turned down Shane's invitations to dinner at Merrick Ranch every time he'd made one, so it made sense that she'd heard about the family's tradition of dressing for dinner. And, going by the times he'd seen her, Nick had to wonder if she even owned a dress.

A slight flush came into her cheeks, but he watched her gaze spark with interest and faint surprise. Her voice was a soft, quiet drawl.

"Thank you for the invitation, Mr. Merrick. Are you…sure?"

He knew right away she was asking if they were still foes, so he smiled to reassure her. "Times change. People change. You're close to Shane. We've been neighbors all your life. Might be time to be a little more neighborly…Corrie. I'd appreciate if you could call me Nick."

He saw the flicker of doubt and thought for a moment he'd overplayed it. But then she apparently bought into the idea of neighborliness and quickly made up her mind.

"I'm obliged. What time should I be there?"

"Seven o'clock's the time we usually set for company."

"All right, seven."

He reached up to tug a pinch of hat brim. "Until then."

## CHAPTER THREE

THE moment Nick turned away to walk to his pickup,
Corrie dashed to the back of the house and the privacy
of the back porch. She left the bucket by the door and
let herself in to sprint through the kitchen and the
house to peek out the front windows.

*Times change... People change...*

As the stunning words replayed in her head, she
watched Nick open the driver's side door and climb
in. She couldn't quite believe the past few minutes
had happened. Or that Nick Merrick had invited her
over for supper.

She couldn't believe she'd accepted! *Why* had she
done that? Because of Shane, she told herself quickly,
not certain she wanted to look beyond that. As she
watched Nick turn the pickup in the drive and head
for the highway, she tried to slow her racing heart.

First Shane had come over and now Nick. Neither
had acted the way she'd come to expect. Had she
imagined it?

*I was thinking it might be a nice surprise for Shane
if I asked you to supper tonight...*

Had Shane said something to prompt Nick to show
such a remarkable sign of acceptance? Not only acceptance of her, but of whatever Shane's feelings for

her might be? Granted, she'd expected nothing more than friendship from Shane. Until today. Today the things Shane had done, the things he'd said, were something more than friendship. How much more?

How much more than friendship did she want?

If she'd been confused and excited over Shane's visit, it was nothing compared to the tizzy she was in for the next two hours. She raced through her chores and hurried upstairs to her room to rummage through her closet and drag out the things she'd bought six years ago.

Most were too formal for a "casual" supper, and that was good because she wasn't sure she had the nerve to suddenly show up anywhere wearing them. Corrie Davis couldn't go from cowhand to debutante in two hours without knocking the world a little off its axis. Nevertheless, she tried everything on to be sure of that, finally putting most of it away.

Feeling desperate and a little anxious, she went through everything else she owned, which wasn't a lot besides work clothes, searching for something better than blue jeans but less dressy than the yellow sundress she'd hung on the closet door to think about. She had a denim skirt, but she rejected it too because it was a skirt.

She hoped the pair of white jeans she'd pulled out and the plain, pastel pink blouse were informal enough to qualify as casual, yet were feminine enough to show her in a little less "mannish" light.

At least they wouldn't look radically different from the shirts and jeans she usually wore.

She'd never worn the jeans and once she'd put them on, she wasn't exactly happy that they were stiff and much snugger than her regular ones. The pink blouse was a simple, long-sleeved tailored shirt, and she carefully folded back the sleeves, then fussed with them to make both sleeves even before she remembered to add a belt with a plain gold buckle.

The few pieces of jewelry she'd bought were only costume quality, but the gold chain necklace and the gold clip-on earrings supplied a hint of sparkle that she liked.

As she looked into the mirror to consider the uncommon notion of maybe having her ears pierced, Corrie was reminded that she'd thrown away whatever makeup she'd had a couple years ago. Aggravated because she had no time left now to rush to town to buy some, she ran a brush through her hair and decided to pull a little of it back from the sides into a barrette, but leave the rest of it loose. She experimented with rolling her lips together to redden them before she gave her cheeks a little pinch and paused to inspect the results in the mirror. It would have to do.

Once she found the shoebox that held a pair of brown leather sandals she'd never worn, she put them on and got out the small brown leather handbag she'd hung on a hook in her closet. It was just as plain as the sandals and had also never been used, so she pulled out the wad of paper and tossed it to the dresser before she slipped her brush inside and added her wallet. She closed the catch on the handbag, lifted the long strap to her shoulder, then stood in front of the mirror for a final inspection.

It was as good as she could manage, and it shocked her a little to realize she'd been at this for close to two hours. Usually, she could be ready for anything in the time it took to brush out and braid, put on her clothes and grab her boots. It was a small consolation that she at least looked as if she'd done more than she usually did. A lot more.

*She looked like she was out to catch a man.*

The horrifying impression jolted her. The last thing she could stand was for anyone to think she was desperate to get a man.

Appalled, she pulled the strap off her shoulder and laid the handbag on the dresser top. She pulled off the earrings, about to toss them back into the old cigar box that held her meager collection of jewelry, when pride reared up.

She worked hard. Damned hard. Never in her life had she pushed herself on any man or chased one, and she never would. She'd never done anything to draw attention to herself, and even if she had, it was hardly a moral failure. She'd barely been kissed, because the only kiss she'd ever had had been a hilarious accident.

The glitter of anger in the gaze that met hers in the mirror made her eyes look jewel bright. However she normally dressed, she was a female. At twenty-four she was a woman. It was no one's business but hers that she qualified for womanhood on account of gender and age rather than some notion of sexual experience.

Why wasn't she entitled to wear pink, put on a little jewelry and carry a purse? Why would anyone be rude enough or cruel enough to challenge her or poke fun? If she'd had any makeup in the bathroom, she'd have every right to use as much of it as she pleased.

*So what* if she wanted to use this occasion to dress and act and *be* more feminine? And maybe even set out to attract a man? Why should she be denied the full right to express a bit of her biological and emotional nature just because she'd waited until some man had finally flirted with her a little before she'd again decided to change something about herself?

Most females had been doing far more than this little bit since before high school. She was long overdue to do likewise. And so what if she wanted to attract a man, marry and have a family? All she'd had of family had been a remote and rarely affectionate father old enough to be her grandfather, who'd barely paid attention and had seldom talked to her about anything besides ranching and markets and the weather.

Having a family one day was her highest and fondest hope, though most of the time she was forced to put it out of her mind. No sense pining for something that didn't look likely to happen soon, if ever.

Her modest effort just now to make up for a little

lost time surely wouldn't register with either brother
as a scheme to nab one of them. If they even noticed
the difference.

And even if they took one look at her and decided
she was manhunting, why would that be so unnatural
and repulsive? There wasn't an unmarried female under thirty-five in their part of Texas, or anyplace else
the Merrick brothers had ever been seen, who hadn't
tried at one time or another to attract them. And probably more than a handful of those women had been
much older than thirty-five.

Feeling better about this, Corrie refastened the earrings, fussed with her hair a little more, then snatched
up her handbag before she started downstairs.

She was more than halfway to the Merrick Ranch
before her tension began to ebb into a heady feeling
of excitement. Not too long after that, the most unexpected question of her life popped into her head...

*Which brother was she most excited to see?*

She slowed the old pickup to make the turn off the
highway onto the Merrick Ranch's main road as she
mentally raced to weigh the answer. Which brother?

The one she was comfortable with, who'd flirted
and given her a sliver of hope for at least the possibility that he—or some other man—might one day
fall for her a little?

Or was it the unattainable brother who'd shown up
that afternoon to invite her to supper?

As she completed the turn and began to accelerate,

nerves and indecision kept the question going around and around...

Was she more excited to see the brother who'd hugged her and taken her boots off, who'd spoken to her more as a female than a pal...the *old friend* whose blue gaze had shown a hint of the naughty thoughts he'd claimed other men thought about her?

Or was she more excited to see the brother who didn't know—and probably wouldn't care—that he could still make her feel as shaky and breathless around him as he'd made her feel at eighteen...the one who hadn't needed to lay a finger on her to do that?

The novelty of the question and the way her mind shifted from one brother to the other and back, magnified her excitement so much that she suddenly realized how pathetic it was to get so worked up over so little.

Maybe she *was* desperate for a man, *any* man. Proof of that was how much she was making of all this. What if Shane had been teasing today? The idea that she could have mistaken being teased for being flirted with made her a little sick.

And she'd always been hopelessly infatuated with Nick. He hadn't needed to invite her to supper for the first time in twenty-four years to achieve that. But his out-of-the-blue invitation had made her irrationally jump to the conclusion that the world—and him in particular—was overdue for her pink blouse and earrings debut.

Shame roared up and beat her down until she felt about two inches tall and unspeakably foolish. And pitiful.

If she hadn't driven close enough by then to see Nick Merrick standing on his front porch as if he'd been watching for her, Corrie might have turned around and hightailed it back home while she thought up some lie to cancel supper.

But he was looking in this direction. He'd surely seen her old pickup and the rooster tail of dust it had kicked up, so she was as good as stuck.

Stuck being stupid and presumptuous and dressed like she was *trying* to look more feminine and attract a man. Stuck, and about to shame herself in front of the two men who'd inspired the foolish fantasies and outright overreaction that accounted for the insanity of the past couple of hours.

Pride wasn't enough to help her salvage even a smidgen of that feeling of entitlement she'd had just a little over a half hour ago, but it was at least enough to help her get out of her twenty-year-old pickup without mussing the clean blanket she'd spread on the dusty seat to protect her clothes.

And though she didn't have enough pride left over to help her hold her head high as she strode up the front walk, she had enough willpower to fill in as she struggled to give the impression that she dressed in pink and white all the time and was regularly invited to eat supper with handsome men.

If she survived the night, she'd dig out every re-

motely feminine thing she owned and burn them tomorrow. Then she'd never be tempted to repeat this
mistake and embarrass herself again. Better to live
alone the rest of her life than to chance being publicly
humiliated. Or worse, cause folks to feel sorry for her.

With her insides churning, it took a lot to meet
Nick Merrick's dark eyes and force a faint smile she
hoped would conceal her embarrassment. Only she
couldn't meet his gaze because it was traveling down
her body in that same skim-and-linger way it had that
afternoon.

A prickly kind of heat shot over her from scalp to
toes and she steeled herself for some expression of
either scorn or amusement. To her surprise, that dark,
almost black gaze came back up and bore into hers
with an intensity that made her feel invaded and a
little weak.

She couldn't detect either scorn or amusement,
though she could see something there. Something a
little like what she'd seen in Shane's eyes that day,
only now she felt breathless and she realized her body
felt uncommonly warm in every place that gaze had
lingered.

Nick's low voice was a gravely drawl that made
the phantom sensation of warmth repeat. "Evenin',
Miss Corrie. I'm glad you're here."

She gave a curt nod. "Thanks for having me."

The stiff comeback was another excruciating little
embarrassment, but if it had sounded wrong or awkward to Nick, he didn't let on. He let her precede him

inside the big house, and she tried to distract herself
from his nearness by having a look around.

The two-story Victorian ranch house that had been
expanded over the years was a showplace. The rooms
inside were large—huge. The dark, high gloss oak
floor of the entry hall had a large reddish-brown wo-
ven rug in the center of the floor that featured a heavy
black outline of the Merrick brand. A wide, carpeted
staircase curved up from the hall to the second story,
and three portraits of what had to be Merrick ances-
tors had been placed at ascending intervals on the
whitewashed wall by the staircase. Four other portraits were situated on the entry walls at eye level.

A hall table sat beneath an elaborately framed mirror to the right of the front door, and the moment
Corrie took that in, her gaze flinched from the reflection of her wide-eyed gaze. She was barely into the
house and she was already gawking like the backward
hick she was.

From there, Nick took her past a formal parlor on
the left and a library. A surreptitious glance into both
rooms revealed plush carpets, elegant wood furniture
with rich amber brocade upholstery and oil paintings
that made both rooms look like pages out of a high-
class decorating magazine. Corrie felt as out of place
as a muddy work boot at a ballet, and wished—heart-
ily wished—she'd not been so wildly eager to come
here.

The big living room Nick escorted her into went
all the way to a wall of gigantic multipane windows

on either side of a set of wide French doors at the
back of the house, which looked out on a large, deep
patio and the swimming pool beyond. Shane had invited her over to swim a handful of times, so she'd
known about the pool, though she'd never come over
to use it.

Shane's father had looked like a fierce, crabby man
whenever she'd seen him, so she'd always been a
little afraid of him. The fact that Jake Merrick had
been in a wheelchair the last years of his life had only
seemed to make him more surly. Shane had often
been at odds with him, so she'd been leery of attracting the man's choler. The best way to avoid that had
been to keep her distance.

Her father had never had much to say about Jake
Merrick, and his dealings with Merrick Ranch had
been infrequent. He'd seemed to tolerate Shane, referring to him as "Merrick's boy," and warning her
not to let that "rich boy" make a fool of her.

Corrie couldn't help feeling a little as if she was
about to be made a fool of, though if it happened
tonight it wouldn't be Shane's doing but her own. It
was at least some comfort that this room was less
formal than what she'd seen of the house so far.

Nick gestured toward the leather furniture grouped
in front of the wall of windows. "Go ahead and sit
down. I thought you might like to look at a video of
one of Shane's winning rides. Unless you've seen it."

Corrie chose a place at one end of the long sofa

just as the housekeeper came bustling in and halted next to Nick.

"Might as well get to the introductions," he said. "Miss Louise? This is Miss Corrie. Miss Corrie, this is Miss Louise. The best cook in Texas." Corrie smiled and they exchanged hellos.

Then Nick asked, "What would you like to drink? We've got just about anything you want. Louise can get it, or if you'd rather have a mixed drink, I can take care of it. And we've got wine, don't we, Louise?" He looked over at the woman to catch her nod.

Corrie's first impulse was to decline all the choices, but it might be rude to do that. If Nick was only being polite and didn't mean to have something himself, she didn't want anything either. It seemed more mannerly to find out what he was having or not having, and follow his lead.

"What are you having?" she asked, then realized she was nervously chafing her palms on the thighs of her white jeans. She made herself stop and clenched her fingers to quell the impulse.

"I was going to mix a drink. Would you like one too?"

She'd never had alcohol of any kind and hadn't wanted any. She didn't really want any now, but she gave a nod. "Whatever you're having."

Corrie caught a glint in his dark gaze that came and went so quickly she could easily have missed it. What did that mean? Was that amusement she'd seen?

Did he realize she was no drinker? It probably didn't take much for him to figure out she hadn't indulged in very many of the adult things he took for granted, like drinking alcohol.

Miss Louise went out and Nick walked to the liquor cabinet at the side of the room and opened one of the doors. The forest of bottles inside looked like a section in a liquor store and Corrie realized she was out of her league on yet another score. Were the Merricks serious drinkers? It wasn't an idea she liked.

Shane had told her about a beer party or two he'd gone to, but that had seemed to be the usual high school jock thing to do in these parts. Her father had kept one bottle of whiskey in a kitchen cabinet, but it had sat for years unopened.

The glassware above the bottles must have been crystal, and she watched as he selected a couple of stout tumblers and set them out, then opened a silver ice bucket and used the silver tongs that went with it to put ice cubes in the tumblers. He picked out a bottle that read Vodka, and poured an amount into each glass. When he finished, he opened a lower cabinet that turned out to be a tiny refrigerator. He took out a glass pitcher of what was obviously orange juice, used the glass stirrer to give the pulpy drink a few brisk turns, then poured some in each of the vodka tumblers.

It seemed like a lot of fuss, and Corrie was surprised that he did it himself, instead of having Louise do it. Her father had been very rigid about things like that, so at least this part made a favorable impression on her.

Corrie liked orange juice, so this might not be such a risk, though she'd heard things about vodka. Surely Nick wouldn't notice she wasn't drinking much if she only sipped from time to time.

And where was Shane? She'd feel far more at ease if he were here, though she didn't think she should ask about him this soon. It would make her look over-eager to see him again.

Nick picked up the tumblers and came her way, handing her one before he sat down in the leather chair nearest her end of the sofa. She give him a slight smile along with a soft ''Thanks,'' before she set the tumbler on her thigh, untasted, and remembered to slide her pinkie finger beneath it to keep condensation from putting a damp ring on her jeans.

''We're just waiting for Shane,'' he told her as he settled back and tasted his drink. He was wearing the same clothes he'd had on that afternoon, so he really hadn't wanted to change into something more formal for supper tonight. She noted then that his stark white shirt had long sleeves that he wore folded back almost exactly the same as hers. She felt a pang of regret over that, and wondered if wearing her sleeves folded was considered more mannish than feminine. She'd never thought to pay attention before.

But when her gaze came back up to his she felt an unsettling ripple of excitement at the dark glitter in his eyes. The white shirt set off his weathered tan and black hair and emphasized his rugged looks. Somehow the way he looked gripped her more now than it had earlier. Enough so that it took her a moment to realize he was still speaking.

"We'd still have time for that video, unless you'd rather wait to see it when Shane's here to give his narrative."

The phone on a side table rang before she could answer, but Nick made no move to pick it up. She hesitated awkwardly until it rang a second time then stopped mid-ring.

As if he'd sensed what was on her mind, he added, "Shane told Louise he was going to Coulter City, but he expected to be back at six. He must be running late, unless that's him now."

*Oh, yes, please let it be Shane, saying he's almost home!* The thought barely finished before the house-keeper came back in.

"Boss?" Louise paused as he glanced her way. "That was Shane. I told him you were waiting supper, but he said he's tied up in town and might not be home till late. He hung up before I could mention he had a guest."

"Did he say where he was?"

"No, sir."

He thanked her and she bustled out. Corrie felt a flash of horror. Shane wasn't coming home? What on earth would she and Nick Merrick talk about? She wouldn't have come tonight if she'd thought it was even remotely possible that Shane wouldn't be here. And now there was no way to get out of this and escape the half dozen potential disasters her brain was suddenly conjuring up.

# CHAPTER FOUR

NICK GAVE her a smile that looked relaxed and unconcerned, as if he wasn't at all troubled by the notion that it would be only the two of them at supper.

"I reckon that's the problem with surprises," he said, reminding her that she'd been invited as a surprise for Shane. "Sometimes they come back at you, though I can't say I have a single complaint this time. Shall we go on in and sit down?"

Corrie gave a tense nod and tried to smile a little, though it felt more like a twitch.

*I can't say I have a single complaint this time.* It was a compliment of sorts, but he'd only said it to make her feel more comfortable about this. That was kind of him and she appreciated it, but she couldn't begin to think of what he could do or say that would make comfort possible. Would she even be able to swallow her food?

Corrie rose to her feet just before he did. She'd meant to start around the long, low coffee table to go toward the wide doorway into the dining room, but he was staring at her in that intent way again, so she paused, feeling a frustrating awkwardness. She could have sworn Nick had been about to say something.

But then he did speak, and she was at least a little relieved that she'd read him right.

"It's something of a family tradition to escort the ladies to the table, so...Miss Davis?"

He held out his free hand and everything inside her went on full alert. There was something about this that she was wary of, but he was kind to maintain his tradition, even though it was only Corrie Davis who'd come to supper.

Nevertheless, it took a lot for her to take that step and put her fingers in his. She hesitated that last second because she was so ignorant she was afraid she'd do it wrong. And she suddenly remembered that her hands were hard with calluses like a man's, and that the backs of them were rough, not soft and lotioned like the delicate female hands he usually touched and would surely prefer.

Her hesitation prompted him to take hold of her fingers. The warm, gentle grip that swallowed hers sent an electric thrill up her arm that went directly from her shoulder to her knees and made them go weak.

But that was nothing compared to the way her heart began to flutter as Nick drew her to his side and tucked her hand in the crook of his arm. She didn't dare look him in the eye, but she could feel the pressure of his gaze on her face. He put his free hand over the back of hers to keep it in place, and she felt a sudden warmth deep down.

His touch was sharply pleasurable, and her body

was suddenly clambering for more. Had she been so
starved for a man's touch that this little bit was making her body go haywire? Or was it because it was
Nick Merrick who was touching her? It was a wonder
she could hold on to her drink.

Thankfully he didn't seem to see evidence of the
absolute earthquake that was going on inside her—at
least not as far as she could tell—as he started them
toward the dining room. She was already miles beyond her life experience, and she felt more than a
little desperate about how much of her backwardness
showed.

And then they reached the dining room, and she
felt a soft jolt of awe. There were two more large sets
of multipane windows and another set of French
doors overlooking the patio, but her attention was
captured by the glossy veneer of the table that looked
about a block long. The three crystal chandeliers
above it were lit, but the scores of tiny lights had been
dimmed, though the mirror finish of the table reflected
every bulb and crystal drop. A matching buffet sat on
one side of the room with a gorgeous set of crystal
bowls. A serving table on the opposite side of the
room had a silver tray and coffee urn bracketed by
silver candlesticks.

Corrie was even more impressed by the three gal-
lery-quality oil paintings. One was a scene featuring
Texas bluebonnets, and the other was of open prairie.
The third was a portrait of Nick's and Shane's
mother. Though Amelia Merrick had passed away

many years ago, Corrie had seen a photograph of her once.

Nick led her to the end of the table where one place setting was at the head, with a second to the right. Flowers and a silver candelabra with unlit ivory tapers sat near the place settings, and Corrie felt even more out of her element.

The candles and flowers seemed romantic to her, but she knew they couldn't be meant that way. Rich folks like the Merricks probably had lots of things that would be special to her, but common to them. And habit. Both the flowers and the candelabra fit in a room this formal.

Corrie tried to make her brain focus on what she remembered from those etiquette books, but when nothing came to mind, she began to calculate how long it would take to eat supper, stay a few minutes more, then beat a swift retreat.

An hour was probably too short a time to be polite, but the way she felt now, she might not be able to survive another five minutes. What if she couldn't think of anything to say? What if her side of their conversation was no more than nods and single syllable replies?

It helped to remind herself that Nick Merrick was smart enough and experienced enough to know she was a hick. He knew he wasn't ''dining'' with some city sophisticate. However gracious he was being with this ''escort the ladies to the table'' tradition, surely he could tell that she was anything but a lady, and tongue-tied to boot.

As long as he didn't guess *he* was the reason she had so little to say, she wouldn't mind at all if he thought she was dull. Meanwhile, it would take determined effort to get down enough food to keep from insulting "the best cook in Texas."

Corrie was touchingly reserved with him, and despite the fact that she ran her ranch as well as a man, dressed like a man, and worked like a common cowhand, there was something so vulnerable and delicately feminine about her that the contrast fascinated him.

And how long had it been since a simple, nonsexual touch from him had made a woman blush? Did he even date women who still knew how to blush? He realized then that he'd become a little jaded, and that the women he tended to go out with these days had long since lost the luster of innocence. Realizing that made him feel almost reprobate.

He walked Corrie to the place set for her to the right of the head of the long table, then took her drink and set it and his own down before he pulled out the chair and seated her. Her beautiful hair looked soft and silky, and he only just managed to keep from touching it to find out for sure. She smelled of some floral shampoo that made him want to bury his face in all that hair, and the strength of the impulse surprised him.

He forced his brain away from that and noticed that Louise had already taken Shane's place setting off the table. She'd also moved the candelabra closer, along with the flowers, which no doubt she'd added because of Corrie.

And as Lou often did when a single lady came to supper, she'd left the lighting of the candles for him, so he took care of that before he sat down. He glanced over at his silent guest and caught the reflected glow of candlelight that made her blue eyes flicker like soft flames. She'd watched him light the candles, and once he'd sat down, she looked over at him and smiled, and he sensed her almost childlike pleasure over the lighted candelabra.

"That's very…nice," she said softly. "And the flowers are beautiful."

"So you like candles." He said it as a fact, because the answer was obvious. "Candlelight becomes you."

Nick pretended not to notice the frank surprise that showed in her gaze for just a second before it veered a little from his. "Miss Lou likes flowers about as much as you seem to," he went on. "Only she prefers having them sent out from town, rather than growing them herself."

"I—I've never grown any that fancy. Just the garden variety," she said quickly, too quickly, because she was probably still reacting to his comment about the candlelight. She gave a small, dismissive shrug then, as if she'd either run out of words or was subconsciously dismissing his compliment.

Nick couldn't help comparing her again to the women he'd dated. Women who were refined and glamorous and self-involved enough to expect compliments, which they received as their due. And not a one of them was half as enchanting as the solemn-eyed woman who sat with her hands in her lap, the pulse at her throat fluttering as fast as hummingbird wings. A woman who seemed so completely unaware of her appeal that he wanted to somehow let her know about it.

But why was it that she seemed so innocent and unaware of how attractive she was? Surely Shane, who had a Casanova's gift for verbal seduction, had showered his girl with compliments? Corrie's innocence came through even more strongly then and struck him hard. Was this a sign that Shane's attraction to Corrie hadn't been a high school romance gone far too serious? Could his father have been mistaken about Shane's interest in her?

On the other hand, Corrie's blushes and tense silences might be because of the things he'd said to her six years ago. He'd not been especially harsh, but he'd been blunt enough to give the unmistakable impression that he considered her lacking. He'd known at the time that he'd hurt her feelings, but he'd figured it was kinder in the long run. His father wouldn't have been as humane.

She might only have come here tonight because of Shane and whatever her feelings for him might still be, but now that Shane wouldn't be showing up, she probably felt obligated to go through this to the end. He gave her credit for that, because she risked giving him another opportunity to say hard things.

Louise came in then, and he caught an inkling of relief on Corrie's soft features. She smiled faintly at Louise as the two made eye contact, but after Lou had unloaded her tray and gone back to the kitchen, Corrie's gaze shifted his way as if she was taking her cues from him.

He reached for his napkin and obliged. "We could use some rain on our side of the fence. How's the water holding out on your place?"

It was a simple enough question, and an inevitable one between ranchers. As he'd hoped, it gave them a start.

The meal actually went fairly well. Corrie had never got over feeling self-conscious, but she'd managed to do justice to the food.

Conversation hadn't been as difficult as she'd feared, and it was something of a compliment that Nick talked cattle and horses and business as if he counted her an equal. And he'd listened to the things she'd said, agreeing or disagreeing, and encouraging her to do the same, so he hadn't talked down to her. At least not that she could tell.

She liked him more than ever as the evening had gone on. He was still the man who'd told her she wasn't suitable for his brother, but it was hard to hold it against him since she'd agreed with him at the time and still did. Realistically, she might never be suitable for Shane. She wasn't suited to Nick either, though it was hard to keep that in mind tonight.

Her infatuation with him years ago had been mostly hero worship, and she'd also thought he was the handsomest man she'd ever seen. He still was. He'd been older and more serious and responsible than the boys her age, and that had impressed her.

She hadn't known him herself, but she'd found out a lot about him secondhand because Shane had frequently talked about him. Though Shane had often resented his brother's authority over him, he'd also admired him.

There'd been times when Shane had confided the details of a dispute between the brothers. But the things Nick had done or said that had riled Shane had often seemed reasonable to her, and when they did, she'd carefully let Shane know she thought Nick might be right.

Looking back, it was amazing that Shane had confided so much in her—and that he'd not resented her for seeming to take sides against him, though he'd always come around to see things the same way once they'd talked it through and he'd finally cooled down.

In her opinion, the biggest problem Shane had ever had was that he had to deal with two strong authority figures—his father and his older brother. And though he'd had an easygoing, more approachable personality, he was at least as driven and domineering as the other males in his family.

Corrie had often marveled over her insight into Shane's family relationships, particularly since she'd rarely had insight into her own relationship with her father. She'd envied Shane's closeness to both his father and brother, despite their frequent disputes. However volatile and headstrong the three of them had been, their conflicts were also part and parcel of the strong and deep allegiances between them. Whatever their private squabbles, at the first sign of trouble from outside the family, they'd closed ranks.

Corrie had never felt loved enough or secure enough to ever think of challenging her father as Shane had his. She'd never been able to confide in her dad either. He'd rarely been harsh and she'd never done without, but he hadn't treated her as much more than an extra pair of hands.

He appreciated that she could put in a full day's work on a nonschool day, but every day she'd cooked, done laundry and taken care of the house. During the school year, she'd been unable to work a full day outside, but she'd done plenty of outside chores before and after school in addition to her regular inside work.

She'd started doing a lot of that about the time she'd turned eight. Her aunt had lived with them until then, but she'd suddenly passed away and her father had expected Corrie to take over the things she'd done. Thankfully, her aunt had been patient enough and determined enough to teach Corrie to do housework, possibly because she'd known her health was failing and that her brother might not bother to hire a housekeeper.

He never had hired a housekeeper, and that had made the loss of her aunt especially hard. Corrie had struggled, that first year especially, to do all the cooking and inside chores. If it hadn't been for the mothers of a couple of her friends later on, she might never had had the benefit of female counsel, especially when it had come to things maturing girls had needed to know. Corrie couldn't remember her mother at all outside of a few old photographs, and her father had rarely spoken of her.

It was a wonder she'd had time for many friends, but she'd managed. Shane had often come over to give her a hand with outside chores so she could do things with friends, and after he'd got his driver's license, he'd given her rides to school events. Their friendship had started during a junior high science project and gone on from there. Over the years, they'd spent more than one evening at her kitchen table studying for a test or working on school assignments.

Their friendship had been uncomplicated by boyfriend/girlfriend attraction, which hadn't surprised her because other boys hadn't seemed to pay attention to the fact that she was a girl either. She'd been too common and too boyish.

Now as Nick let her precede him out the French doors that opened onto the back patio, Corrie despaired of being just as common as she'd ever been and, despite her modest efforts tonight, still being more boyish than feminine.

The infatuation she'd had for Nick seemed to have multiplied and expanded the past hour, but the hopelessness of it made her feel impatient with herself. And restless. It was a strange kind of restlessness that seemed to make her skin feel hypersensitive.

Nick hadn't offered his arm as they'd left the table to go outside, so they were probably done with his family traditions. It might have been nice to have one last little thrill to take with her, since she doubted she'd ever be alone like this with him again. If there was a second invitation to a surprise supper for Shane, it would be Shane who would handle that particular tradition.

Nick's low voice interrupted her thoughts as he closed the door behind them. "I thought you might like to see some of the flowers we have out here and around the house. There's a purple clematis you might like to have a start from, and probably a few other perennials you would be interested in. My foreman's wife takes care of the outside flowers here at the house, so I could tell her which ones you choose. I'll bring them by when it's convenient."

The offer was another surprise, and she looked away. "You don't have to do that."

"Why not? My mother loved swapping plants. She gave away almost as much as she brought home," he said as he started them across the patio stones. "I don't remember that she ever bought flowers from a greenhouse unless it was something new that nobody had yet.''

Corrie glanced his way and saw the calm smile he gave her, as if he knew she wasn't sure how to take his offer. And that she might be too proud to take something for free from him.

''If you think you owe me something in exchange, then let me pick something from your flowers when you have me over for supper one night this week.''

Corrie had started to look away from him to the purple clematis that covered a wide trellis at the back of the pool area, but her gaze shot back to his. She must have looked just as surprised as she felt, because his smile widened, and the harsh ruggedness of his face softened into genuine handsomeness as he went on.

''Although along with supper, I might rather have some tomatoes from the garden I noticed while I was at your place today. You've got quite a green thumb.''

Corrie stared a moment, her surprise slipping close to shock. And then she realized she was almost as thrilled by this as she was a little appalled. Thrilled because Nick was inviting himself to her place, with no mention of Shane. As if he'd enjoyed tonight and wanted to repeat it.

But she was appalled because she'd just seen the inside of Nick's fancy house and knew her little place would come off mighty poor by comparison. Shane had always been comfortable there, but she might have been more far squeamish about inviting him inside that first time if she'd seen for herself how grand a house he was used to.

Corrie looked away from Nick and faced forward, feeling the same confused excitement she'd felt with Shane at noon that day. Maybe she'd got knocked on the head when the colt had tossed her off that morning, and the whole day since had been some sort of crazy dream. Wonderful, but crazy. And not really happening.

Because unless this was a delusion, Nick Merrick had just invited himself to supper at her house. *This week!* On the other hand, it was only polite to pay back a supper invitation with a reciprocal invitation. She hadn't needed to read that in an etiquette book because it was common politeness and she'd regularly done it with friends.

But those friends worked and lived pretty much as modestly as she did, so no one paid much attention to what others had or didn't have because it was friendship that was important.

On the other hand, Nick knew she didn't come from money and that she didn't pretend to be something she wasn't, namely rich and sophisticated. He surely understood he wouldn't be sitting down with her in some elegant dining room with oil paintings on the walls or silver or fine china or expensive crystal.

The fact that he seemed to want to sit at her modest table and eat her cooking was actually quite a compliment.

An amazing compliment. Perhaps one of the nicest compliments she'd ever had, because it might be *her* he wanted to see and spend time with. Then again, she might be making more of this than she should, which told her more about herself and the lonely way she'd lived than she wanted to face.

# CHAPTER FIVE

CORRIE slowly came to a stop beside a row of planters that were loaded with blossoms.

"Wh-which night?" she heard herself asking.

She'd never been a coward, but having Nick over for supper would perhaps be the greatest act of courage in her life. She'd thought coming here tonight had been nervy enough. Now she had an opportunity she would have given anything for at eighteen, and she couldn't think of not taking it, no matter how it turned out.

"If not tomorrow night," Nick said, "then the next night. Or the next." He gave her a smile that slanted a little. "It's rude to invite myself, but I've enjoyed tonight. I hope you'll overlook the bad manners of wanting another night."

Now his smile widened and her heart fluttered wildly. "My, my, Miss Corrie. You look like you think I might be up to no good."

She felt her cheeks go warm. Nick's gentle teasing reminded her strongly of Shane, and the similarity gave her a wisp of ease.

"Are you?" she dared softly. "Up to no good?"

"If I am, I'm confident you'll set me straight."

Her warm cheeks went warmer. Was that a reference to her tomboyishness? As if she'd spoken the question out loud, he gave her an answer.

"According to my brother, you managed to keep him in line. You taught him a very valuable lesson in manners, at least once that I know of. Remember?"

Corrie couldn't remember offhand any time she would have taught Shane manners, because Shane had always been well-behaved. Then again she was flustered, so it was a wonder she could remember yesterday.

"When did I do that?"

"Let's see," he said and then looked at some spot over her head, as if trying to recall the exact details before his gaze met hers again. "The two of you were probably in eighth grade, and the time I remember involved homemade slingshots and a piece of tin you'd nailed to a fence post."

Corrie felt a bubble of laughter come up, because she suddenly remembered it too. She turned away to start walking along again, ignoring the flowers as that time came back to her. She and Shane had been shooting rocks at their target, but she'd hit it nearly every time while Shane had only managed to hit the target about half as often, even after they'd traded slingshots. He'd finally thrown his slingshot down, declaring it was kid stuff.

Offended that her friend was discounting their competition—and by inference, her skill, just because *he* wasn't winning—Corrie had boldly accused him of being too spoiled and "sissy" to lose to a girl.

Shane had fumed over that, snatched up the slingshot, and promptly missed the target a few more times. He'd ended up throwing the slingshot as far as he could and cussing a blue streak.

Nick supplied his memory of the story as he strolled at her side.

"Shane came home wet and mad as a hornet. He admitted what had happened, then he claimed you shoved him into a water trough and told him to go home and wash his mouth out with soap. You informed him that you were just as much a female as any other girl, and he'd better watch his 'cussin'' around you. Oh, he was *red hot*."

Nick chuckled, and Corrie tried to keep back a mortified little giggle, but couldn't. She looked over at Nick's smiling profile, hoping he was as amused by what she'd done as he seemed. "So he told you about that."

"Me and our daddy. Then he suffered the added indignity of having both of us laugh at him. Until then, he'd never lost competitions with any real grace, but getting dunked in a water trough was the beginning of wisdom for my kid brother. On that subject as well as the subject of swearing around the ladies."

He looked over at her then, his dark eyes lit with laughter and an approval that made her feel something akin to joy.

"You were the first kid in his life who wouldn't put up with a poor sport, and you were apparently not going to stand for being 'cussed' at."

"I remember being worried after he stomped off," she told him. "Shane's horse almost bolted because he couldn't stop yelling, and then I had visions of your father coming over to talk to mine."

Nick shook his head. "He needed the lesson. The one about sportsmanship stood him in good stead on the rodeo circuit, and he can still cuss a blue streak, but only when the ladies are out of earshot." He gave her a speculative look. "I know he decided he owed you an apology. Did you get it?"

Corrie smiled at the memory and faced forward as they reached the part of the patio where the pool was. Shane had apologized, sincerely, the very next time they'd seen each other in town. Then he'd taken her to the diner on Main Street for a hamburger and a malt, and they'd been closer friends than ever after that. Shane had never used swearwords around her again, and he'd never allowed anyone else to either.

"He apologized," she said, belatedly realizing she'd been lost enough in the memory that she hadn't answered yet. But she kept the details to herself because they were ones she treasured. It had been the first of many times Shane had taken her for a hamburger or to a movie. There'd not been anything romantic about it, but she'd enjoyed going with him every time. "He was a good friend."

"And then during your senior year, more than a good friend."

Nick's statement sent an arrow of unease through her that struck deep. There was something different in his low voice, something serious she couldn't quite identify, except that it felt wrong somehow.

Had he said that because he was fishing for confirmation of something romantic between her and Shane all those years ago? Even if he'd believed that at the time, surely Nick could tell from the years she and Shane had barely had contact that there'd been nothing like that between them. And still wasn't.

She shrugged a little, uncomfortable.

"I never understood why you thought Shane and I were anything more than friends," she said with soft candor, then stopped and looked over at him.

He stopped walking too, and she inwardly cringed at what she'd just said. Nothing like baldly bringing up the one conversation—if that one-sided encounter could be called a conversation—that she hadn't wanted either of them to mention tonight.

"What about now?"

His low question and the utter seriousness in his gaze banished any remaining illusion of ease or neighborliness between them, and Corrie felt a little sick. And shaky. Was this what tonight had really been about? To find out how things were between her and Shane? No sense beating around the bush.

"Is that why you had me over tonight? To find out?"

Nick gave a solemn nod. "That's how it started."

Corrie felt a little shakier and glanced away a moment, trying to take this in, knowing without a doubt that it had been a mistake to take any of this as she had. She should have stuck to old habit and avoided Shane's home and his family like the plague.

Oh, how suddenly the lovely evening had changed, and she'd been too foolish to see it coming. She'd taken it all so seriously, as thrilled as she was worried that she was imagining how well things had gone. Nick had genuinely seemed to enjoy having her over, discussing things with her as if he credited her with both a brain and an opinion worth hearing. How much of *that* had been real?

Probably none of it. Obviously Nick had just been stringing her along, luring her into a false notion of neighborliness, subtly flattering her ego until he could get to what he'd really wanted. The idiocy of thinking for even a second that the very worldly and experienced Nick Merrick might be interested in her as a woman—how else would *any* female have taken his mention of coming to dinner at her place tomorrow night?—was especially low-down. The shame she felt over being so easily taken in made her insides twist.

He'd certainly gotten her to make a fool of herself, and her shame over that was something she wouldn't get over for a while. It took a lot to make herself look him in the eye.

"Shane was never going to be here, was he?" Her normally slow temper began to kindle and rise as that occurred to her. The gaze that stared into hers was somber.

"I did mean for Shane to be here. I just should have told him before he went to town so he wouldn't have found something else to do. But yes, I wanted to see you together. I figured I'd find out what I wanted to know without asking.''

Her chin went up a little. "I have a couple questions of my own then, and I'm not too chicken to ask them. Number one, why is it any business of yours? And two, why not just ask Shane?''

She saw the flash of anger in Nick's dark gaze and knew her little barb about being too chicken had hit home. No doubt it was especially offensive coming from someone like her. She took what small satisfaction she could in that because it was probably the best thing she'd get out of tonight, besides an education.

In the long run, it wouldn't matter how Nick answered either question, because after tonight she didn't intend to ever have a thing to do with him. He no doubt felt the same way, and probably had all evening. How hard had it been for him to pretend to be such a gracious host?

A harshness came over him then and she was reminded of that day six years ago. "I see it as my business because it could affect the future of Merrick business. And Shane doesn't discuss you. He closed that subject years ago.''

It was a brisk, blunt, efficient answer that told her everything she needed to know. Corrie gave a stiff nod. "I have no idea what I'd have to do with Merrick business, unless you're afraid Shane might marry so far beneath himself, but if there's something your brother won't discuss with you, maybe you ought to respect his silence.''

She couldn't seem to keep the slight tremor of anger out of her voice, but that was fine because she wanted him to know she meant every word. Particularly since it didn't take much imagination to figure out how talk about her came to be off limits. ''The next time you want to know something about me, show us both the respect of asking straight out instead of pulling another stunt like this one tonight.''

Corrie turned and strode away from him. There was no need to even go back into the house, since her keys were always in her pocket. Any effort she'd made tonight to behave a little more femininely was overwhelmed by the need to leave Merrick Ranch by the most direct path, as swiftly as she could and still maintain some dignity. If her stride was too long to be ladylike, then too bad. Tonight had put an end to any ambitions on that score.

Corrie was untroubled by the sound of bootsteps that eventually started after her as she stepped off the edge of the patio at the back corner of the huge house and stalked across the lawn to the front driveway.

She didn't look back as she reached the old truck, got in, switched on the engine, then turned in the driveway and shoved down the accelerator.

By the time she got home, she was so riled and stirred up, and so unsure about how she'd reacted to Nick there at the last—had he really been that dastardly?—that she came as close to tears as she had in years.

She'd just yanked off the gold earrings and hurled them across the kitchen, not caring that they hit a cabinet and ricocheted around the room, when she heard a pickup engine coming around the back of the house. Though only friends drove to the back, she immediately concluded it was Nick.

Corrie reached on top of the refrigerator and switched on the radio, then turned up the volume a little. From where she stood she could see through the thin curtains on the back door as a tall cowboy shadow came up the porch steps to loom just outside. The shadow opened the screen door then a hand came up and knocked on the inside door, which aggravated her because she couldn't make herself ignore it.

The idea that Nick had followed her home was upsetting because she couldn't figure why he'd do that. Did he want to apologize? But if he'd wanted to do that, he'd had enough time to call her back and get it done while she'd still been at his house. It was more likely that he had other things to say, things she was sure not to like.

On the other hand, she could think of another thing or two she'd like to say to him, so she might as well take this opportunity to get them said. Corrie stormed over to the door and yanked it open.

Only it wasn't Nick standing on her back porch, it was Shane. The smile he'd had slipped away as his gaze moved from her anger flushed face and went down the front of her. A slow grin came over his mouth and he gave his head an equally slow shake.

"Boy howdy, Miss Corrie. You look like about three flavors of ice cream. Vanilla pants, strawberry shirt, and chocolate hair into next week." His gaze came back up to hers and he narrowed his eyes a little before he gave the kind of low whistle usually reserved for stark amazement.

"And you're mad as blazes, aren't you?" He studied her a moment more, nodded as if he was doubly certain of it, then warmed to the subject.

"Oh, yeah. And it's about a man, gotta be a man. So who is this hombre? Or maybe I should ask, who's the low-down, dirty skunk who got you so riled?"

Not for anything would Corrie say a word to Shane that would identify his brother. She didn't want anyone to ever find out she'd gone near Nick Merrick or Merrick Ranch. And Shane hadn't figured out she was angry about a man because he'd read her mind, not when she was dressed so differently than normal. He'd simply put one and one together and made a lucky guess.

"I'm mad at the world, cowboy." She made the effort to calm herself and blew out a tense breath. "But I'll cool off in a while."

Corrie stepped back in a silent invitation for him to come inside. "What have you been up to?"

Shane walked in, taking off his Stetson as he did to upend it on the kitchen table while she turned off the radio. He hadn't taken his hat off when he'd come by that day, so Corrie couldn't help noticing that he did it now, as if he was reacting to her more feminine pink blouse and white jeans.

She saw him glance at the floor, saw him do a double take, and knew right away he'd seen one of her earrings. Corrie cringed, regretting her rash, angry impulse. Shane walked toward the discarded earring and bent down to pick it up before he glanced around and spied the other one and got it. He straightened and turned to set them on the table without comment, though she could tell he wanted to. Instead, he answered her question.

"Been out seeing what's new in town, and got a look at the new Country bar on the highway," he said before his gaze went down the length of her again and Corrie felt a new kind of heat in her cheeks. "Been there yet?"

Was he fishing for information too? Somehow she couldn't fault him, not after he'd seen the earrings and seemed to understand why they were on the floor. After all, he'd just guessed she was furious over a man.

"I don't go to beer joints," she said, and Shane chuckled at that.

"Just because they serve beer doesn't mean it's a sin palace, Corrie. They've got about every kind of soda you'd want. They've also got a halfway good Country band tonight, and a big dance floor. I came by to see if you'd like to go dancing."

"I don't dance."

He grinned. "Well *I* do, Miss Mad-at-the-World Grouch, and I can give you a few lessons if you can keep from grumbling at me long enough." His gaze traveled over her again. "Nah…change that. You can grumble all you like and I'll still teach you to dance."

He nodded at her shirt. "Pink suits you to a T," he said, then grinned as his gaze again floated downward. "And I've lived to see the day that Corrie Davis put on a pair of tight, white jeans." His gaze went all the way to her feet. "And sandals. You've got cute little toes after all, don't you? You probably show 'em off all the time now."

Corrie was so stunned she couldn't speak. She'd felt so wounded by her foolishness tonight that Shane's little compliments were sorely welcome and they softened some of her worries about the way she'd dressed tonight. She at least trusted enough in their old friendship to be certain his compliments were sincere.

Shane's gaze came up slowly, stopped at her hips as if he was noting the feminine flare there, then lifted to settle on her waist.

"All you need now is a good belt with a big shiny buckle to show off that nipped-in little waist. A bigger one than that little belly button bead you've got on now," he added, referring to the small round buckle on her belt. "Here…"

He reached for his gold, world champion buckle to unfasten it and strip the belt out of his jeans loops.

"My belt's too long for your itty bitty waist," he

said as he walked closer, starting to unsnap the buckle from the leather.

Appalled, Corrie impulsively reached for his hands and gripped them to make him stop.

"Oh, don't, Shane! Put it back on. Please."

Shane's gaze shot up to meet hers and her breath caught at the look on his handsome face. Corrie felt his hands slowly turn and grip hers. She was looking up at him and he was looking down at her, with only their hands between them. The backs of her fingers were pressed against his warm, hard middle and the backs of his rested just below her breasts.

Suddenly something changed in him, something more serious than she'd ever expected.

"I'd like you to wear it tonight, Corrie," he said quietly.

"I couldn't, I—it's yours to show, not mine. I won't go if you don't wear it yourself."

One side of his handsome mouth kicked up. "Then you'll go dancing with me tonight?"

The question made her eyes sting, and she wasn't sure why.

"I...don't know. But please, you earned this the hard way. It wouldn't be right for anyone else to wear it. I'm no world champion bronc rider," she said, then tried for a little humor to coax Shane out of his seriousness. "Ask the colt that dumped me this morning."

Silence rose around them those next seconds as he

looked down into her eyes and she looked up at him. His voice went a little raspy.

"You're a world champion woman, Corrie," Shane said slowly as if he was making a pronouncement, and she almost couldn't bear to keep her gaze on his because she was suddenly struggling to hold back sentimental tears.

"Stupid me," he went on, "I just realized that, and I can't figure out why I didn't know it years ago. I guess I want to give you something to say so."

A nervous little laugh slipped out of her, and she shook her head, desperate to deflect what he'd said because she was truly about to cry. "Did they hand out gold buckles for world champion flattery on that rodeo circuit?"

Shane's face went even more serious "No, ma'am. Flattery is insincere. I was paying tribute. Big difference."

Corrie lowered her chin to look down at their clasped hands. If she could just go back to that morning. Things had been simple then, and dull. But she didn't know how to deal with anything that had happened from the moment Shane had called out to her from the back porch. Since then, she'd been moved so far beyond the things she understood and knew how to handle that she might as well be standing on the moon.

As she watched, Shane released one of her hands and took away the buckle and belt to lay them on the kitchen table behind him. Then he brought his hand back. But instead of taking her free hand, he placed the side of a finger beneath her chin to coax her to lift her face.

She only had enough time to see the utter solemnity on his handsome face and register the electric intensity of his blue gaze before his dark head started a slow descent.

She barely got out the words, "Oh, Shane… don't," before his firm lips touched her slightly parted ones with no more pressure than a butterfly wing. And then that butterfly touch lifted, came back, and lifted again before it settled a last time and let her feel the slightest bit of warm weight.

Corrie felt as self-conscious as she was shocked, but ignorance distracted her. Should she kiss him back? Should she close her lips? Should she turn her face away?

Shane relieved her of the decision when he drew back a little. His low voice was a rasp.

"Am I kissing another man's woman?"

The question jolted her. The answer came gusting out in a breathless, "No, of course not," that was nothing but the raw truth.

"Of course not?" He chuckled. "What's that supposed to mean?"

The low sound of his voice carried an undercurrent of disbelief that gave her a bittersweet little ache. But it was time to stop this, all of this. She'd been royally hoodwinked by one Merrick brother, and she wasn't about to even wonder what this Merrick brother was up to.

Maybe the worst part of what Nick had done was to put doubt in her mind about all men, including Shane. Shane was a friend, but she didn't trust herself not to take this the wrong way or to make more of it than Shane might mean. He was probably an expert with the ladies and kissed women all the time, so this was nothing special to him.

Corrie made herself step back and would have pulled her hands from his if his grip hadn't gently tightened to keep hold of them. Corrie couldn't look him in the eye.

"It's been a really long day, Shane. I'm so tired I can't think straight."

He chuckled again. "That 'can't-think-straight' feeling is because of the kiss, darlin'. If it's not, I'd be happy to try again."

Corrie made herself smile, though his confidence about the effect of his kisses could only mean that he'd had tons of experience giving them, so it wasn't necessarily a compliment to hear that he thought she was reacting predictably.

"I'm glad you came home, and I'm glad you came by. It's been a long time."

She forced herself to look up at him and prayed she could get him to leave now. The memories of the time when they'd been in eighth grade—and about a million other memories—were coming back so strongly, along with the love and gratitude she'd had

for him as a friend, that her heart was full of sentimental feelings.

So full she felt like bawling. The kiss had only
magnified all that because it had changed something
between them, and she wasn't sure it wouldn't somehow eventually hurt their long friendship. She was
just too worked up. The best thing for that had always
been to get some sleep.

Shane looked down at her as if he suspected something, but in the end, he let her have her way. Except
for the kiss he'd planted on her cheek on his way out
the door, there hadn't been anything else.

Corrie took a moment to pick up the earrings from
the table, then briefly debated throwing them in the
trash. In the end, she turned off the lights and took
the earrings with her as she went upstairs.

# CHAPTER SIX

CORRIE realized the moment she couldn't find her best hairbrush that next morning that she'd left her handbag on the sofa at the Merrick ranch house. She'd carried a purse so rarely that she hadn't given it a thought. If her wallet hadn't also been in that purse, she would have just replaced the brush and forgotten about it.

She gave up on her other brush and instead used a wide-toothed comb and did the best she could with it before she braided her hair and dashed out to do a few early chores before she came back in for breakfast. Her two part-time ranch hands came to work at about six-thirty. Today they were moving cattle to another pasture, so she wanted to be ready before they got here.

She could hardly call Merrick Ranch and have Shane bring the handbag over, because she didn't want him to know she'd been there. She didn't worry overly much that Nick would tell Shane about it because there were apparently other secrets between the brothers that involved her. Maybe after things had gone wrong last night Nick would be just as eager as she was to keep her visit a secret. Miss Louise would probably do whatever Nick asked so Corrie had to think of another way, besides through Shane, to get the purse back.

She couldn't chance going over when Shane might be there, and she hated the idea of facing Nick again on his own turf. Since she'd never been one to sneak around, she wasn't sure how to handle this. The last thing she wanted to do was cause trouble between the brothers. She already knew from Shane that there were enough tensions over Merrick Ranch and his need for independence.

Besides, Shane had witnessed her upset last night, and because he had, she couldn't let him find out that the low down dirty skunk he'd asked about was his own brother.

Particularly since she was having second thoughts about what Nick had done. Yes he'd invited her over for reasons other than he'd led her to believe. But there'd also come a time when he'd admitted it. She just wished he'd volunteered the information before she'd asked outright. And yet, he'd owned up to what he'd done the moment she had, and he'd told the details. Maybe he had truly meant for Shane to be there, just as he'd said.

If she hadn't been so stupidly thrilled to be with him, she might not have reacted so strongly. It probably wasn't too hard for a man like him to figure out that she'd reacted as strongly as she had because she'd taken his polite attention too seriously. And in a way he couldn't have intended.

And that only reinforced the idea that her inexperience in male/female things disqualified her from venturing into that frustratingly mysterious realm. Better to stick to what she knew and understood. If that left her in lonely limbo, at least she wouldn't make a complete fool of herself, and her pride would stay intact. At least what pride she had left after last night.

The low feeling that had dogged her the past few weeks came back with a vengeance, and this time it brought with it a stinging sense of cowardice that outraged the very sense of pride she wanted to protect.

In the end, the best solution for her was to work.


"Hey, big brother, I've got a question for you," Shane said as he and Nick sat down to breakfast.

Nick was in no mood for his brother's early morning cheer, but it wasn't fair to inflict his dark mood on Shane. They'd both got a belly full of that when their daddy had been alive. "What's that?"

Shane reached for his napkin, dropped it onto his lap, then reached for the meat plate.

"Do you hear talk of who's seeing who in these parts?" he asked as he helped himself to a slice of meat then handed over the plate.

"Sometimes. Who?"

"Corrie Davis. Who's she going out with these days?"

Nick felt his dark mood deepen. "Why?"

"Just askin'."

Like hell he was just asking, but Nick didn't sense

that Corrie was as sore a subject with Shane as she'd been in the past, so he didn't want to make her one again. He wished he hadn't practically ensured that last night. "I thought talk of Corrie Davis was off limits."

Shane dumped half a platter of eggs on his plate, then handed it over too, a little of his early cheer slipping.

"Talk of *me* and Corrie Davis is off limits. That and the kind of discussions our daddy wanted to have. Ones that were variations on, 'That Davis girl isn't good enough for a Merrick.' And, just for the record big brother, bad talk about her of any kind is still taboo."

"Then why bring her up and chance what I'd say? The only reason I was ever interested in her was because of you. Back then, and now."

A little more of Shane's cheer dimmed. "Let me change the subject the tiniest bit, then we'll circle back to Corrie. Who was that gal you fell for a few years back? Old Yancey Edwards' oldest daughter, but I can't recall her name offhand."

"Jenna? I didn't fall for her. We were *seeing* each other."

"That's the one. You made me dig fence posts in a drought for a solid seven days because I said just one time that Jenna Edwards was all looks and no brain."

Nick couldn't help the smile that pulled at his mouth as he remembered that. "You didn't have to dig fence posts because you *said* it to me. What got you the punishment was because you said it to me when her daddy was standing close enough to hear.''

''So you admit now that it was true?''

''It was true.'' Nick had no problem saying so. Jenna Edwards had turned out to be all fluff and no substance, with only a passing acquaintance with common sense, thanks to a daddy who'd made life too easy for her and spoiled her rotten. The point had been to teach Shane to keep his opinions to himself when the wrong folks were in earshot.

''So now we'll circle back to Corrie,'' Shane said then. ''What you and Daddy said about her was never true.''

''I don't recall that I said much about her outright.''

''Daddy said to my face at this very table in front of you that Corrie Davis was the kind of girl you felt up and fooled around with in the hayloft, but she wasn't the kind to show off to your friends and marry.''

Nick had forgotten the specifics until now, but after spending the evening with Corrie, he understood now how profoundly insulting—and untrue—their daddy's remarks had been. ''He was out of line, and you know I told him so at the time.''

''Yeah, you did. But you also told me a girl like her wouldn't be able to hold my attention for long, so I'd better be keepin' my pants zipped.''

"If you'll recall, I said it to you about every girl you dated."

"The only time you sounded deadly serious about it was when it was Corrie you meant. Like she wasn't good enough to carry Merrick seed."

"If she was good enough, then why did you go on the circuit without her? Why didn't you marry her?"

"She was a friend, Nick. That's what was so unfair about your attitude and Daddy's. It wasn't in my head to play slap and tickle with her or to have a roll in the hay. Hell, she was so naive and innocent that only a pervert could have looked at her and thought of sex. It made me mad that you and Daddy made something dirty of her."

Maybe they had done that. In their daddy's case, it had been meant to. In his case, he'd been thinking at least a little about Corrie Davis. She hadn't had the best life with her old man. And he'd worked her like a dog. She might have been tempted to jump out of the frying pan into the fire of a teenage marriage. Living in a house with another old man who'd been so bitter and in pain that he'd lashed out at everyone, would have given her nothing but misery, particularly if his little brother had lost interest in her.

If Corrie had followed Shane off to college, she would have felt sorely left out, though if she and Shane had married, Nick would have seen to it that she was enrolled too. But Shane—and Corrie—would never have heard the end of it from their daddy.

"I didn't mean to do that," Nick told him. "I was

worried male hormones and proximity might make a mess of your life and hers. And an innocent like Corrie, who gets seduced and then dropped when the boy loses interest, gets hurt. Even if you'd gone too far and later married her, you know living under this roof was no picnic either back then.''

Shane was hunched over his plate, thinking that over, all traces of cheer vanished. While he did, Nick searched his conscience. Had he said worse things about Corrie that he didn't recall? Had he *thought* worse things about Corrie? He honestly couldn't remember anything.

He did however have something bad enough to own up to, and he might as well tell Shane now. He'd probably have a hell of a time getting Corrie Davis to listen to an apology, and if she wouldn't, he might need Shane's help.

Nick made a start toward his confession. "Is Corrie still only a friend?"

Shane gave him a level look. "She and I have grown up a lot, so lots of things have changed. Maybe that too. I reckon I'll find out soon enough. But just remember, Corrie Davis is no slut and she's not Jenna Edwards."

Nick smiled a little at the contrast between the two as he set his fork down. "No, going by my impression, a woman like Corrie wouldn't sleep with a man she wasn't married to, and no, she's not remotely like Jenna. To answer your question about who she's seeing, I doubt she's seeing anyone."

Shane hadn't shown a reaction to his "going by my impression" remark, but it was time to get this in the open. Nick took a sip of his coffee then looked directly at his brother as he set his cup aside.

"From what I saw last night, if there is someone she's interested in, it's probably not too serious yet."

Shane's gaze sharpened. "Where'd you see Corrie last night?"

"I invited Miss Davis to supper to surprise you. But when you called Lou, you hung up before she could tell you about it. You didn't tell her where you were either, so I couldn't call back."

"Then Corrie didn't come over." Shane sounded certain about that.

"She was here when you called."

"She was, huh?" Shane put down his fork and sat there a moment, his forearms still resting on the table. "I could never get her to come near this house." He smiled a little as if he was amazed. And pleased. "Corrie came here for me? What did she say when I didn't show up?"

"Not a lot. She's very shy. It took a while for her to relax, but once she did, we had a good time. Or maybe I should say, she *seemed* to have a good time. I know I did. She's polite, pleasant and very knowledgeable, a thinking woman who knows how to say what she thinks."

Especially at the last. It dawned on him now that they'd been standing by the pool when she'd told him off. He was lucky he hadn't ended up dunked like Shane had years ago.

"So the two of you got along?" Shane seemed especially happy about that. Nick hated to tell him the rest, but it had to be done.

"Well enough that I invited myself to supper at her place."

Shane's grin eased a little and he casually leaned back a little more. "Is that right? Huh. What did she say to that?"

"She asked me which night I wanted to come over," Nick said, then paused to note that Shane's approval of the story had dimmed to almost nothing, and he saw more than an inkling of what could only be jealousy in his brother. Well, Shane could relax.

"But it wasn't too long after that when I said a couple of things that spoiled it."

Shane gave him a narrow look. "What things?"

"Are you sure you want specifics?"

"Hell, after a lead-in like that, you're damned straight I want specifics. And I saw that girl last night, probably right after she'd got home. I've never seen her that mad about anything—*I've* never made her that mad. I wondered who the low-down dirty skunk was, but I've got the feeling we're talking more about horse anatomy than critters."

Shane's mouth twisted into a grim smile. "So, big brother, how much of a horse's backside were you?"

It was past noon before Corrie put her horse away and got back to the house. The cattle were moved, the men were gone, and the heat had sapped the edginess and nerves she'd felt that morning. That was just as well when she caught sight of the tall, harsh-looking rancher who was just walking around the side of her house to the back. With her handbag.

Her upset last night and that morning, and her dread of facing Nick again, was defeated by the foolish thrill of seeing him walk toward her. Though he was dressed for outdoor work in a blue plaid shirt and wash-worn jeans, he was so impressive and overwhelmingly masculine that she couldn't seem to help the ache she felt just looking at him.

Shane was more smoothly handsome, and much more dear and familiar, but it was Nick who truly affected her. Maybe it was because he was so much older, and so much more experienced in the work and the rough, outdoor life she also dealt with day to day. Even when he'd been much younger, Nick had always seemed adult.

Maybe he'd never really been a child, just as she'd never really been a child. There had to be some common, unremarkable reason she'd always been drawn to him.

And because she was such a boyish female, maybe it was just natural to respond to a man who was as harshly masculine as Nick was. After all, she'd grown up competing with boys in just about anything requiring physical skill and strength, and she'd never felt romantically attracted to any of them. It was hard to imagine she'd ever be attracted to a man she felt physically equal to. Not that she wanted to be dominated, but because something in her craved the kind of security a strong man seemed to promise.

No sense wondering about any of that though. Better to just accept that Nick made her feel things she'd have to ignore. Better still to get her handbag back and deal with whatever more he might say. Or not say. Then he'd leave and she'd go into the house. They'd rarely crossed paths in the past, and they'd soon be back to doing the same.

Corrie felt sweat trickle down her forehead, probably cutting through a layer of dust. Just before she reached Nick, she reached up a hand and brushed it away, hoping she'd managed to wipe both sweat and dust off without making a mess.

"I see you found that," she said, careful to sound casual. "I'm obliged to you for dropping it by." She hoped that gave enough of a hint that she didn't expect him to stay. She didn't want to be rude, she just wanted this to be over quickly.

The last thing she wanted was to feel obligated to invite him inside or to loiter around in the yard talking. What would they say to each other anyway? Nick handed her the purse and she reached to take it.

"I was wondering if we might talk," he said, and she felt her insides begin to flutter. The little inner twang had started pretty much the instant she'd seen him, but she'd tried to ignore it. She wanted to ignore the added persuasion of his soft question, but she had to struggle to do that.

And then he reached up to take off his black Stetson. The ''hat in hand'' gesture suggested things that flattered her female ego. Particularly when he held it between his big, strong hands and slowly rotated it. As if he was nervous. Corrie couldn't help searching his dark, dark gaze to see if that was true. He went on while she tried to decide.

''I enjoyed having you to supper, Miss Davis. My initial reasons for inviting you over last night were wrong, and I apologize for that and for being dishonest about it, but those were the only things I was dishonest about. I don't regret having you to myself last night or getting to know you a little. As I said, I enjoyed that. I never meant any harm or offense to you, so I hope you'll consider accepting my apology. It's sincerely made.''

The low speech went straight to her heart and kicked it into a rampaging gallop. Her face felt on fire and she suddenly couldn't maintain eye contact with his somber gaze. If he was faking, he ought to go to Hollywood and make movies. He'd be a star overnight.

''I...thank you,'' she said, dismayed that her voice sounded husky, and she felt almost overcome with bashfulness. Before she knew it, she'd yanked off her hat and spanked it against her thigh. It was a masculine gesture of agitation, and she was instantly mortified to realize she'd done it, particularly since she held the purse in her other hand.

But she *was* agitated, mostly because his apology crowded her and practically demanded something more than a simple thank-you. And the intensity in him had short-circuited her brain so she had even fewer ideas about what to do or say next than she might normally have had.

"You're still put out with me, aren't you?" he said, but it was more a statement than a question.

Corrie made herself look at him then, frustrated enough but now even more frustrated that she'd given him the wrong impression. The words gusted out of her in a candid rush.

"In case you didn't notice, I'm about as backward as it's possible to be and still get through the day. I'm put out with my own clumsiness. No wonder you were worried your brother might marry me." She gave her hat a wave and put it on. "And now that we've covered that, I'll say thanks for bringing the bag and thanks for the apology. Everything's put right, so I'm going in now. Goodbye."

Corrie moved around him and strode to the house, feeling the excruciating pain of thorough humiliation. It was entirely self-inflicted humiliation, and somehow it felt more acute because it was self-inflicted. The tiny bit of relief she'd expected to feel for being so starkly honest about herself would take some nurturing. A *lot* of nurturing. But for now, she wished the ground would crack open so she could just dive in and disappear.

Nick's low masculine voice seemed to grab her like a giant's fist and brought her to a sudden halt just short of the porch steps.

"I'd still like to come to supper, Miss Corrie."

Had she heard right? Did she dare turn to see if he was still standing there and not walking in the side yard to where he'd parked his truck?

She glanced back over her shoulder to see that he was still there, and now he was watching her as if he expected some kind of response. "Why would you want to?"

"How many reasons do I need? I enjoyed last night, enough to repeat it. And enough to rudely invite myself to supper a second time."

The smile he gave her was fully male and staggeringly sexy. "And you're an attractive woman. Should I list something else, or is that enough to explain why I'm hoping you'll have me over for dinner? If you don't want to cook, I'd be happy to pick you up. We could drive into Coulter City for supper, maybe catch a show."

Corrie faced forward, almost defeated by doubt and wariness. And then doubt and wariness—and outright disbelief—declared victory. She didn't look back as she gave him her answer.

"I'm busy the next two nights. If you'd still like to make plans for some other night, you're welcome to give me a call."

She rushed up the porch steps and went inside, so ashamed of her infernal ability to act and talk like an ignorant clod—but so glad to get out of Nick Merrick's sight—that she started a whirlwind of housework that didn't end until late that night. Though she took what time she needed to do evening chores, by the time she finally ran out of nervous energy and fell into her bed, her sleep was both deep and mercifully dreamless.

## CHAPTER SEVEN

CORRIE hadn't planned to go into Coulter City that next morning, but the special feed mix she'd ordered for one of her yearling colts had come in and she was eager to see if the new feed would solve his problem keeping on weight.

It might do her good to go out and be around the usual folks, and spend some time in town picking up a few other odds and ends she'd need sooner or later. She badly needed some perspective on what had happened the past couple of days, and she wasn't getting it by herself.

It was all going around and around in her head, no matter how much she tried to put her mind on other things. Her brain was already keeping track of how many hours were left in the two days she'd given Nick, and that was particularly upsetting.

*If you'd still like to make plans…you're welcome to give me a call.*

What a simpleminded thing to say! As if she was some social butterfly with so many men lined up to eat her cooking that her calendar was full. She was lucky he hadn't laughed his head off.

Why she couldn't simply forget he'd ever asked was another testament to how foolish she was. And how easily enthralled she'd always been by Nick Merrick. The word enthralled wasn't a common one for her, but its meaning, "to hold spellbound", was pitifully accurate.

The common sense that had ruled her life seemed to have flitted away somewhere, as if it had turned just as cowardly as she suddenly had in the face of a real challenge. And in the absence of common sense, her heart was prey to thinking impossible things, things like maybe finding out a little more about what it would be like to be with a man in a social situation and not make a fool of herself.

She'd worked with men for years and thought nothing of it. She'd never had dinner with one, not a man and her alone, until two nights ago with Nick. There'd always been others around, friends with husbands or a group of ranch hands or ranchers. Shane didn't count from years ago, because they'd been friends. She and Nick weren't even that.

As she went into the feed store and made herself look around, she finally began to make progress getting Nick off her mind. She loaded the feed herself, then drove down the street to the hardware store for a couple other things on her list. When she walked out, her gaze fell on the big front window of the dress shop across the street.

She actually got in her pickup and put the key in the ignition before her gaze strayed back to the mannequins. One wore a flared denim skirt and a red peasant blouse with an elastic neckline that stretched so low around her shoulders that it rested on the mannequin's upper arms. Another wore a blue sundress with wide straps, a shirred bodice and a flared skirt.

She remembered that scrunchy look was called shirred because she'd read it in the magazines she'd bought years ago. One of the mannequins wore a slim, white linen dress that was sleeveless but casually dressy, and another was wearing a bodice-hugging, seersucker dress in multicolor pastel stripes that cinched in at the waist then flared out into a skirt that gave it a carefree summer look.

The clothes were a bit less fancy than the ones she'd bought in San Antonio, and since they were new, they might be more up-to-date style-wise. Though she'd been careful to find classic styles back then because she'd wanted them to last so she'd get her money's worth, there was something appealing about the ones in the window.

And she couldn't seem to forget the look in Nick's eyes when he'd smiled that sexy smile and told her she was an attractive woman. She might have automatically rejected that if not for the things Shane had said. Because of Shane, she had some sense that maybe she wasn't so plain anymore.

What if Nick did call her? And if a miracle like that happened and she was brave enough to have supper with him again, what would she wear?

Should she go into the dress shop and have a closer look, maybe try something on? Or would it be another small splurge on clothing she'd never wear? The moment she realized how idiotic it was to think Nick would really follow through, she rejected the idea of repeating the nonsense she'd indulged in six years ago.

Nick Merrick would never call. She simply wasn't the kind of female a man like him would bother with, though he'd bothered with her to a stunning degree already. Whatever his reason for doing that, she was certain it was connected to Shane. Because men like Nick didn't pay attention at all to women like her unless there was some reason that had very little to do with the woman herself.

The tap-tap-tap on the passenger side truck window startled Corrie out of her thoughts, and she glanced toward the sound.

Eadie Webb gave her a wave, and Corrie slid over to reach across the bench seat to roll the window down.

"Hey there, Eadie. I haven't seen you for a while."

Eadie grinned. "I was about to say the same to you, stranger."

"I just came in to pick up a few things."

"Me too," Eadie said, and nodded toward the dress shop window across the street. "Then I saw that Carla Mae has some new dresses in her window, so I thought I might wander in and look around. No tellin' when I'll be in the mood to try something on again."

Corrie smiled a little. Eadie was a small rancher like she was, with pretty much the same outdoor lifestyle. But Eadie did dress up from time to time.

"I thought about it," Corrie said, then grimaced as she added, "briefly."

"Why don't you go in with me? Try on a few things, live a little. I'll take you to lunch afterward, my treat."

It had been a long time since she'd spent any time with Eadie, but Corrie didn't really want to try on clothes. Eadie had already guessed that, and gave Corrie a teasing smile.

"Oh, come on, Corrie. Please?"

Eadie was one of the few friends that Corrie felt completely unselfconscious around. It might be good to try something on, if for no other reason than to hear what Eadie would say about how it looked. Eadie was a year older than she was, so it felt natural to take her common sense wisdom seriously. And Eadie would be honest, so maybe she'd find out what she truly looked like in something besides work clothes.

Ten minutes later, Eadie had picked out an armload of clothes to try on and pulled another armload off the racks for Corrie. Though Corrie was leery of this, Eadie was excited, and she couldn't help catching some of it. After all, she didn't have to buy anything and it might be fun to see what Eadie chose.

They pretty much had the fitting rooms to themselves, and Corrie had the novel experience of trying on clothes then stepping out of the changing stall to show what she'd put on and have a look at what Eadie was wearing.

Eadie's coloring was the same as hers, though

Eadie's hair was only shoulder-length, and since they were virtually the same height and size, they ended up trading a few of the clothes. The hour or so Corrie had thought they'd spend in the store, somehow stretched to three. Eadie's influence and enthusiasm had even persuaded Corrie to buy a few things.

Corrie felt good when she and Eadie walked out of the dress shop and went to the shoe store down the street to repeat their trying on marathon. Being with Eadie had given her a tremendous boost in self-confidence, and thanks to Eadie's comments and suggestions, Corrie no longer felt like a hick tomboy playing dress up. By the time they'd stowed their purchases in their respective pickups and got to the diner, it was after three o'clock.

Once they'd ordered, Corrie's casual, "Are you still working part time for Hoyt Donovan?" made Eadie wince.

"For now."

Corrie studied her friend's face a moment, trying to decide if Eadie was upset or merely annoyed again with the handsome rancher. Yes, Eadie worked part-time for him, but she'd made no secret of her disapproval of his dating habits.

"Is he hard to work for?" Corrie probed gently.

"Not when he sticks to the usual home office chores," Eadie told her as she tore open two sugar packets at once then dumped the contents in her iced tea. "His bad moods are easy enough to deal with. If I don't feel like putting up with them, I leave. It's when he involves me in his extra-curricular activities that I wonder why I ever thought I needed the extra money.''

Corrie remembered Eadie had told her about those. Eadie ordered flowers for his dates but when Hoyt decided to part company with a girlfriend, he enlisted Eadie to select a nice piece of jewelry.

Eadie sighed. ''Lately the 'parting gifts' are getting to me.''

''You aren't comfortable telling him to take care of those things himself?''

Eadie looked down to trace a line in the condensation on her glass. ''No. The first couple of times he asked me to do it, I was impressed that he was thoughtful enough about breaking up with someone that he'd send them some little token. I might have shown a little too much approval, so maybe that encouraged him to keep on doing it. But it's happening too often lately, so often that it's bothering me. A lot. I've made a few negative comments hoping he'll take the hint before I have to say something stronger, but I haven't actually been able to make myself tell him outright. And he's been pretty grouchy lately.''

''Do you think he might fire you from the regular work?''

''No, I'm sure he'd never do that, but he's been acting different, so maybe I have some doubts.''

Eadie was quiet a moment, and she'd stopped drawing lines in the condensation. ''The real truth, ugly as it sounds, is that I feel useful to him, that he needs me. That no matter how gorgeous his women are and how many relationships he has, I'm the one he relies on and can't get along without. It's probably all he'll ev—''

Eadie cut herself off, blushed and looked away. ''Oh, that sounds pathetic when I put it into words.'' She gave an impatient wave of her hand and sent Corrie a flustered look. ''Forget I said that.''

Corrie's soft, ''Okay,'' seemed to relieve Eadie, who rushed on to another topic. But Corrie recognized that sad little gleam in Eadie's eyes. It was clear her friend had feelings for Hoyt, deep ones, and that had to be hard, particularly when Hoyt was only interested in gorgeous debutantes and party girls.

Eadie was pretty, very pretty, but she wasn't flashy like the women Hoyt dated, and she certainly wasn't a party girl. Hoyt Donovan hadn't impressed anyone as the kind of man who would settle down and marry anytime soon, so Eadie probably felt as hopeless about something coming of her secret feelings for Hoyt as Corrie did about her feelings for Nick.

But it had to be awful for Eadie to work for Hoyt several times a week, knowing he'd never see her in a romantic way, much less to also be the one in charge of sending Hoyt's women flowers and ''parting gifts.'' On the other hand, it wouldn't be safe for Eadie to ever get Hoyt's attention because he was sure to break her heart just as he had the others.

Corrie had only a nodding acquaintance with Hoyt, so she'd never had much of an opinion about him one way or the other. Until now. Hearing this made her think Hoyt Donovan truly was a shameless womanizer and yet, if Eadie had feelings for him, he had to have some fairly impressive qualities or Eadie wouldn't give him the time of day, and she'd never work for him.

Corrie wondered then how much she would do for a man she had a crush on. Certainly Eadie wasn't doing anything wrong, although perhaps Hoyt wouldn't have so many ex-girlfriends if he had to take care of his own "parting gifts."

The irony of her thoughts brought Corrie up short. As if *she'd* know anything about male/female relationships, whether good or so-so, fleeting or long-term, since any notions she had were strictly theory. Nevertheless, she felt a little closer to Eadie because of her confession. Perhaps Eadie could give her advice on some of her own little mess.

But only if anything more happened. As things stood, nothing more would happen with either of the Merrick brothers. She hadn't heard from Shane since the night before last, and she didn't expect to. Six years was a long time to be out of the habit of regularly dropping by like he had when they'd been in school, and he had a lot to deal with now. No doubt the brothers were working out their differences over Nick's plans for Shane, and that was something she hoped to stay clear of anyway.

The dresses and shoes in her pickup were the fruits of Eadie's influence and maybe a tiny bit of wishful thinking, but at least she could wear them to church. Before she'd made the final decision about them and written out the checks, she'd vowed to actually wear the things she'd bought this time. If the only place she got to wear them was church, so be it.

After they finished lunch and went their separate ways, Corrie started the drive home. The benefit of having a late lunch was that she wouldn't be hungry enough to bother cooking supper. And without cooking, there'd be nothing to clean up. Since it was nearly six when she got home, she took her new things into the house then drove the pickup to the barn to unload the feed and start the evening chores.

The regular chores went quickly, and when she finished, she put the sack of new feed in a steel barrel, cut open the top of the sack, then measured out some for the colt before she closed the lid and tightened the rim. She'd already put out feed for the other three yearlings, and the leggy sorrel seemed to know the extra feed was for him. The moment he saw her walking toward the colt pasture, he left the others and came to the fence.

Corrie bent down and slipped through the rails, then leaned back against the fence post and propped the shallow bucket on a rail to tip it forward. The colt gave her a sniff, accepted a pat, then inspected the bucket's contents before he began to nibble. While he did, Corrie scratched his ears, content to let him eat while she watched the other colts.

The sound of a pickup engine carried from the house and she glanced in that direction in time to see the big blue supercab pickup she recognized as Nick's pull around the side of the house and come to a halt.

The leap of excitement she felt was disheartening, and she immediately decided to stay where she was. When he stepped out and walked to the back porch, she felt the insane little twang begin to vibrate in earnest.

She'd told him to call, and counting last night, this was the second night that she'd told him she'd be busy. He was supposed to call, so he shouldn't have shown up here anyway, and yet he had. Even worse, she didn't know what she should do about it.

As Corrie watched him and noted the pale blue shirt he was wearing and the dark denim jeans he had on, she couldn't help but enjoy the sight of him, however common the clothes. His wide-shouldered, lean-hipped build wasn't that much different than a million other men who worked the land, but none of those others had ever made her feel this peculiar ache.

Corrie remembered as clearly as if she was touching him now, how her hand had felt in his, and how the iron muscle of his arm beneath the cotton cloth of his white shirt had felt beneath her fingers and palm. She might never forget the hard, welcome feel of the hand he'd placed over the back of hers, and she wasn't sure she wanted to. The warm swirl that went through her middle at the memory was almost as strong as it had been the other night, but brought with it the first sharp edges of misery.

Why was he here? She didn't dare speculate because her heart was already pounding with foolish hope.

Corrie watched as he bounded up the porch steps and knocked on the back door. He waited a moment, then knocked again, hard enough for the sound to drift toward her. A few moments later, he turned and crossed the porch to go down the stairs, his black gaze doing a quick sweep of the area. It lingered on the spot in front of the barn where her truck was parked, so he'd surely expect her to be home.

Corrie stood absolutely still, hoping the tall post she leaned against and the plank rails were enough to keep him from easily picking her out of the landscape. She felt as much as saw it when his gaze slipped over her then snapped back, and her heart fell a little.

Her childish ploy hadn't worked, and she felt more than a bit guilty for hoping it would. Or did she? But there was no sense rushing out to embarrass herself again, or to in any way imply she was eager to see him.

Though she *was* eager to see him and—counter to any shred of common sense—thrilled he was here, there was no reason for him to catch even a hint of that. Especially because she didn't know why he'd shown up.

He'd started walking toward her the moment he'd

caught sight of her, so she pretended not to notice his approach. It was another childish pretense, but sudden nerves had brought with them a feeling of edginess that moved through her and sent that odd, prickly sensation over her skin. She mentally checked herself to decide if any of that could possibly show.

When the colt lifted his head from the bucket and focused on Nick's approach, she was compelled to look in his direction.

Seeing him out here did little to make him look smaller or less blatantly masculine. Corrie's insides were quivering, and the harsh, so harsh set of his face made those quivers carry a thread of anxiety.

But the harsh set of his face softened, and her anxiety dulled the same amount though it still made itself felt. He called out, but his long stride brought him to the fence before he finished speaking.

"I was hoping I might catch you at home, Miss Davis. I was by earlier."

Corrie ignored the foolish excitement of the idea that Nick had come here twice in one day just to see her. This couldn't be about her. "I haven't seen Shane today," she told him, "and it's been a couple days since I have."

"Shane's out with the boys tonight. I came to see you," he said, and the faint rasp in his low voice made her insides grow warm.

"Is something wrong then?" She didn't trust the way the look in his dark eyes reached through the fence and felt like a touch. He was experienced enough to bamboozle females like her, and it was a fact that she didn't know better than to misinterpret this.

He smiled a little. "Not a thing. I had an idea about tomorrow, and I wanted to ask you about it."

The colt began lipping her shirtsleeve, so Corrie moved her arm and put out a hand to give him a little push away before she bent down and slipped through the fence rails with the bucket. Her delay in commenting telegraphed her skepticism. At least she hoped it had. But there was something in the way Nick looked at her that let her know she hadn't succeeded. She'd have to try harder.

"I've got to finish up a few things," she said, then started for the barn. "You can tell me about it while I do."

Nick fell into step beside her and before she realized it, he'd slipped the bucket from her fingers to carry it for her.

"I'm flying down to San Antonio tomorrow to buy a stallion. I thought it might be a more natural opportunity for you and I to spend some time together and get better acquainted. I know you appreciate fine horseflesh, so you might enjoy going along."

They walked into the barn and Corrie glanced over to see his dark eyes on her face. "Why?"

His hard mouth curved a little. "Do you know how much of a challenge you are?"

Corrie reached to take the metal pail from him to set it inside the feed room and pull the door closed, but she didn't answer right away. Instead, she strode to the ladder to the loft and quickly climbed up into the heat that lingered under the wide roof. She picked a hay bale, then dragged it to the edge of the loft floor and looked down.

Nick had watched her go up and now he backed away so she could toss the bale to the floor. She did the same with a second bale before she climbed back down the ladder. By then, Nick had shoved the bales against the feed room wall.

Corrie had been trying to decide how to deal with this, or at least what to say to him. She still didn't have a good idea, and that same sharp frustration she'd felt with him before began to cut through her again. She might as well be blunt and spare them both.

"Look, Mr. Mer—"

"Nick." The curt correction wasn't harsh, though it was instant.

"I might be ignorant about a lot of things, but I know what my bank balance is and I know what I see in the mirror. I'm not the kind of female men like you usually keep company with. Why are you so dogged about this?"

Nick reached up and nudged his black Stetson back a bit, as if he needed that time to choose his words. His black eyes glittered down at her.

"You aren't like the others, and I'm at the place in life where the usual isn't half as interesting."

Corrie stared, certain he was making fun of her somehow though there was something in his dark gaze that she trusted. And yet she couldn't trust it.

The words from years ago that had drifted indistinctly at the edges of her every thought the past three days were suddenly clear in her mind. She'd always remember them in her father's toneless drawl because the words had been his.

*Don't let that Merrick boy make a fool of you... Boys like that don't want the plain ones for more than one thing... Don't be like your aunt, lettin' some randy rich boy sweet talk you into shamin' yourself... You'll need to do for yourself cause no man's gonna help keep a roof over your head as long as there's a pretty girl to be found somewheres else...*

Those comments and more, muttered here and there from the time her body had started maturing, cruel words that masqueraded as fatherly advice, and yet a lot of them had been proven completely true by the boys she'd grown up around. And then Nick had unknowingly confirmed the meaning behind her father's words when he'd let her know she was unsuitable for Shane, which had pretty much closed the issue. The only thing that hadn't proven out were the "randy" boys. And even that confirmed the other things her father had said.

After her father had died, the words had somehow

drifted to the back of her mind because she'd accepted them so completely, but they'd been the bedrock of her thinking about herself. She'd made a life for herself that had never taken her even remotely close to triggering them again. Until Shane had come home.

Though the words hadn't come this clearly into her mind for years, they'd undermined her at every step since the day she'd seen Shane on her back porch. Were the things her father had said still true? Though she had a little evidence now to suggest they weren't—at least not to such an extreme—it wasn't as if men other than Shane and Nick had seemed to notice.

Nick's low voice prompted her to say something. "Well?"

Corrie rubbed a damp palm on the hip of her jeans and looked away as she spoke the truth she was sure of. "I don't know what to say to something like that."

"How about, 'Yes, Nick. I think I'd enjoy flying down with you tomorrow'? Unless you don't like to fly. We could drive down."

She heard the smile in his voice and looked at him to see it was there and that his rugged face was especially handsome. Her heart was suddenly fluttering like a trapped bird.

It seemed as if everything in the universe had suddenly crowded in on her and was bearing down. Her father's words made another circuit through her brain, but something in Nick's dark eyes made her was a little less convinced they were true.

The fleeting memory of Shane's kiss the other night—it shocked her to realize she hadn't thought about it since then—boosted those fledgling doubts about what her father had said, and made her a little less wary of Nick.

The last thing she wanted was to make a fool of herself, and yet it suddenly seemed important that she do something about this invitation. As backward as she felt, this might at least be an opportunity to learn how to handle herself around a man in a different way than she was used to.

This thing with Nick wouldn't last long, and probably nothing more would happen with Shane, but there might be some man sometime who might take an interest in her. It might be good to figure out a few man/woman things before then. Or to at least have some kind of date experience.

She'd meant for her soft, "Yes, Nick, I think I would like to fly down to see that stallion tomorrow," to sound a little more lighthearted than the somber way it came out. And her, "What time?" was more a humiliating squeak than actual speech, but Nick didn't appear to notice either thing.

"How about eight o'clock?"

Corrie muttered some kind of agreement then walked with him to his pickup, wondering every step of the way how she could possibly take more time away from the ranch without getting too far behind in the work plans she'd made for that week.

And she'd never been much farther off the ground than the back of a horse or the hay loft, except for roof repairs, so she had no idea if she'd like flying or not. At least for a while those thoughts helped keep her mind off her real worry: that tomorrow could easily turn out to be the granddaddy of personal disasters.

## CHAPTER EIGHT

THOUGH the few things she could do seemed inadequate, Corrie did everything she could to make certain going with Nick wouldn't be a disaster. The first thing was to call Eadie.

Eadie had been excited about her problem and enthusiastic about helping her, so they'd discussed what to wear and made plans over the phone. Eadie arrived at six-thirty that next morning, bringing with her a modest collection of makeup.

There wasn't time to do much experimenting with the cosmetics. Since they both agreed that only too much was worse than none, by the time they'd finished, Corrie wore a faint hint of eye shadow and just enough mascara to highlight her eyelashes and eyes. She was leery of fooling with lipstick.

"Didn't I tell you those indigo jeans and shirt made your eyes even bluer?" Eadie crowed. "And you almost didn't buy the concha belt and jewelry to wear with them."

Corrie was glad now that she'd bought the silver belt and the plain silver necklace and concha bracelet that matched the belt. She was also wearing her good black boots, reasoning that if they would be looking at a stallion, they'd be out in a barn or corral.

Eadie had agreed that everyday work clothes weren't good enough for today, but the indigo outfit and silver jewelry would be better than the usual, a touch dressy, but still in the range of casual. And not a problem in Nick's small plane.

Besides, Corrie wasn't sure she wanted to go around for hours in anything that felt too different from the comfortable clothes she usually wore. All she'd have to do is remember not to rub her eyes and be careful she didn't catch the bracelet on something.

She'd also have to remember to keep track of her handbag, though she'd slipped her wallet in her back jeans pocket along with a hair tie in case she had to tie back her hair for some reason. Eadie had agreed she should wear it down, but without pulling any of it back into a barrette.

"You make me wish I hadn't cut my hair," Eadie said as she reached over to adjust a skein of Corrie's hair before she stepped back and looked Corrie over. "You look beautiful, Corina Jean." Eadie's mouth quirked. "I wish I cleaned up half as good as you do."

Corrie rolled her eyes briefly, then gave her friend a somber look. "You're the one who's beautiful, *Edith Regina,* cleaned up or not," Corrie said then smiled over their mutual use of given names. "Thanks for this."

"You're very welcome, but do us both a favor and have your eyes checked next week," Eadie said as she started Corrie toward the door.

"There's nothing wrong with my eyes," Corrie informed her, but Eadie ignored that to say, "Buy some glasses."

"Ooops," Eadie said just before they got to the hall door, then went back to pick up a couple things off the dresser.

"Put this eye shadow in your bag," she said, "and here's the compact. If you forget and rub your eye, you'll want something better than a pickup mirror. And speaking of pickups, I'd better get going before Nick gets here."

They went out of Corrie's bedroom then downstairs to the kitchen. Eadie walked ahead of her to the back door and opened it before she glanced back.

"If I haven't heard from you by five, I'll come over and take care of your chores."

"I'll probably be home long before then, but thanks for that too. I owe you some pretty big favors."

Eadie grinned. "My pleasure. Have fun today."

"I'll try."

Eadie went out and she'd driven away barely ten minutes before Corrie heard another vehicle come up the drive from the highway. She peeked out one of the front windows to see Nick's pickup slow then turn back to face toward the highway and stop.

Nick stepped out and she saw he was wearing a royal blue Western shirt with a bolo tie and dark jeans. Apparently they'd both be wearing blue, and she didn't know if that was good or bad.

Corrie dashed to the hall closet for her good black Stetson, then hastily rushed to the front door to set it on the foyer table with her handbag. She was so nervous that her hands shook, and she had to force herself to walk to the door before she could chicken out.

She was rattled enough to open the door just as Nick had been about to knock, and she felt her face flush when she saw the surprise in his dark eyes. His hand froze in midair for a scattering of runaway heartbeats. Then it shifted to the brim of his black Stetson and he swept it off.

The surprise in his eyes had evolved into a gleam of what she now recognized as male interest. His gaze slipped down the front of her to her boots, then traveled back up and pierced hers.

"Your eyes look about as blue and deep as a mountain lake under a clear sky. You're beautiful."

Corrie's heart fluttered with shock and pleasure and mistrust. She suddenly couldn't look him in the eye. And then a little giggle bubbled up and out so quick she couldn't stop it. Mortification made her whole body go red hot. She heard the smile in his voice.

"What? Did that sound silly?" The smile in his voice matched the smile on his face when her wary gaze shot back to check before it arced away.

"Oh…well, no." She had to fight the kind of bashful smile she hadn't had to cope with since childhood. "Just…it was…a little too extravagant to be about me."

"No one's ever said that to you before?" The disbelief in his voice sent a whisper of sadness through her heart and she forced herself to smile a little.

"I think I know now where your brother learned flattery."

"Truth should never be mistaken for flattery."

She glanced at him again then away. "You don't have to do that."

"Do what? Compliment you?" He went on before she could answer. "Are you ready to leave?"

Corrie was relieved he'd changed the subject because he'd put her a little too strongly on the spot with both the compliment and the small challenge.

"Yes." She turned to reach for her Stetson and handbag, then walked out the door. Nick pulled it closed then took her elbow to escort her to the pickup. The electric feel of his strong fingers through the fine cotton of her long-sleeved blouse made her feel warm all over. The swirling feeling had started in deep places, and she felt her breath go shallow.

Had she almost spoiled things back there at the door? Corrie vowed then that she wouldn't act like a giggly child again. A man was taking her with him for the day, and though she knew she wasn't beautiful, she looked the best she'd ever looked in her life, thanks to Eadie. This was an opportunity she couldn't have imagined a week ago, and she was darned well not going to mess it up.

It was high time to be a grown-up woman instead of a backward teenager in an adult body. As far as she could tell, Nick Merrick meant her neither harm nor disrespect. And he was a man of the world, so he probably knew not to expect her to be like the so-phisticated women he usually had around.

Just the fact that he'd invited her along on what was essentially a business trip suggested he might have far more confidence in her than she had in her-self. He must not think she had the potential to em-barrass him, and she prayed that was true even as she vowed to live up to his faith in her.

He opened the passenger door of the tall vehicle and kept hold of her elbow as she stepped up. It was a small disappointment when he released her and she sat down. He closed the door with a snap and she set her handbag and Stetson aside to reach for her seat belt. After Nick got in and started the engine, he buckled his seat belt then smiled over at her.

"Thanks for coming along, Corrie."

Her soft, "Thanks for inviting me," sent a gleam through his dark gaze before he faced forward and put the vehicle into gear.

After they arrived at Merrick Ranch, they drove straight to the airstrip. Corrie had been too preoccu-pied last night and that morning to give a thought to the idea that it would have been simpler and much less trouble for Nick if she'd driven herself to the airstrip.

And now that she was actually about to fly for the first time, she was both nervous and desperate not to show those nerves. Nick seemed competent, and his confidence made her relax a little. Once they were in the air, his deep voice came over the headset.

"We'll fly over your place and let you have a look around," he said then banked the small plane. Corrie's stomach lurched sickeningly, but she made herself look down on the land. She located the highway, and automatically factored the position of the sun and began to watch for landmarks she might recognize that would let her know when they flew over the boundary fence.

Nick pointed out a few things to keep her oriented, which was just as well because it all looked so different from the air that she was having problems keeping track. Within moments, she located her house and the barns and corrals and then watched as the aerial view of the landscape meshed with her ground level knowledge. Her place didn't look very big, especially not compared to Merrick Ranch.

After they flew over the last of Davis land, Nick turned the plane toward San Antonio. At least her insides began to calm a little and slowly adjust to the odd motion of the plane.

They touched down later on a small public airstrip near San Antonio, and Corrie was relieved to arrive on solid ground. Nick had seemed to enjoy her wide-eyed awe and her questions, and he chuckled at the relief she must have shown once he'd taxied to a stop and switched off the engine.

"It was a little bumpier flight than usual, so don't

let this first time put you off," Nick said. "It might go smoother on the trip home."

Corrie made herself smile, though the idea that he'd guessed she wasn't gung-ho about flying made her feel a little guilty.

"It's no reflection on your piloting skills," she told him. "And I liked the view."

"Give it time," he said, though Corrie doubted there'd be another time after they flew home. Nick removed his headset and took hers when she handed it over.

Nick got out first, then turned to give her a hand after she'd put on her hat and slung the strap to her handbag on her shoulder. Corrie didn't do too badly until she'd actually made it to the ground, but when he released her hand she swayed and grabbed for his arm.

Just that quickly, he'd caught her free hand and pivoted so they were face-to-face. The sway had been so momentary that any unsteadiness passed the second after he'd caught her.

"Pardon me," she said. "I think I put a foot wrong."

Corrie let go of his arm and tried to take a half step back, but Nick's hands dropped to her waist to keep her where she was. The surprise of that made her look up.

There was something so still about him, and she might have been a little alarmed at the almost granite harshness of his face if his dark eyes hadn't been glittering down at her with the same intensity that she suddenly felt.

It was like coming in contact with a bare electric wire, and she felt her insides go shivery and warm. The hard fingers at her waist were firm but gentle, and the easy male strength of them communicated something so masculine and dominant that she felt everything feminine in her submit. Nick's low voice was a gravelly rasp.

"I reckon we'll have to deal with this at some point."

*Deal with this?* Even she wasn't backward and naive enough to misunderstand what he was talking about. Corrie felt her heart quiver with both fear and anticipation. This time she managed to step back, and she wasn't certain whether she was relieved or disappointed when he immediately released her.

From there, they walked to the hangar and Corrie found the restroom to freshen up while Nick signed off on a car that had been sent for his use. It was a Cadillac, and she was wowed again by the leather luxury inside the expensive vehicle.

It took ten minutes to reach the ranch they were headed to, and another five minutes before the main house and stables came into view. When Nick pulled up to the front walk, the owner walked out to greet them. He was tall and angular and dressed like a common cowhand, which put Corrie instantly at ease.

"Merrick. Good to have you come down," he said,

then swept off his Stetson to reveal a very bald head. "And who's this pretty lady?"

Nick made the introductions. "Miss Corrie, this is Colby Blake. Colby, this is Miss Corrie Davis."

"Howdy, Miss Corrie, welcome to the Slash B. It's a pleasure to have you come along with Nick, a real pleasure."

Corrie smiled and shook his hand when he offered it, then murmured a quiet thanks.

Instead of walking to the stud barn, Colby took them in the supercab pickup parked nearby. Since the truck had a bench seat, Corrie sat between the two men and kept silent while they talked quarter horses and breeding. Colby drove on a roundabout route that took them past corrals and small pastures where other horses were kept, and he frequently stopped to point out one horse or another.

Corrie couldn't seem to focus on any of them. Nick's arm rested on the seat behind her, and he sat close enough that her upper arm grazed his side. Heat radiated from him and she felt the gradual release of tension in her body as she succumbed to the pleasure of his nearness. She was all but melting. Would she be like this around any man she was attracted to? Or did it have more to do with the fact that she'd been infatuated with Nick so long?

Whatever his interest meant, she couldn't possibly keep it for long, so that and her inexperience probably heightened her reaction to everything now. It struck her then that at least some of what she was feeling might be the result of an abnormally strong attraction to unattainable men.

Considering her very distant relationship with her father, it was possible that the reason her heart had fixated so intently on Nick was because he was, realistically, just as emotionally distant from her as her father had been. It was as if her heart was compelled to recreate some version of the hurt of the past in hope of a better outcome this time. But why set herself up for what could only be inevitable disappointment?

Surely she wouldn't—couldn't—do that to herself, could she? Perhaps it was just the pressure and unfamiliarity of this situation that was prompting her to look at things far more critically than she might have otherwise. That and the fact that Nick's nearness made her body react as helplessly as iron filings to a powerful magnet.

Corrie tried mightily to ignore the foolish sensations going through her body and fixate on the beautiful horses beyond the white-painted rails of the corrals they passed on their way to the stud barn. When they arrived there, Nick again helped her out of the truck before his hand settled on the back of her waist for the short walk into the barn.

Once they were inside, it took a few moments for her eyes to adjust from the brightness outside to the lower level interior light so she could see into the huge stall that took up a fourth of the building. The stallion inside was a glossy red sorrel, and his quarter horse confirmation was picture perfect.

Though he behaved well when a stable hand snapped a lunge line on his halter and led him outside to a round pen, the animal was spirited and the barely contained volatility in him was palpable.

The big horse seemed to have a good temperament but Corrie knew well the unpredictability of stallions, which was why she'd never kept one. Because she was alone a lot of the time, the last thing she needed was to have an energetic and unpredictable stallion on her hands to keep exercised and occupied. She paid stud fees to service the mares she bred.

Nick had plenty of people working for him, so he didn't have that limitation. He also had the thousands and thousands of dollars that enabled him to buy such a high maintenance animal, though from the looks of the stallion, the animal was worth every penny. The Merricks had always raised superior horses, and this horse would be right at home in Nick's breeding program.

Though she kept up with the breed, Corrie dealt with horses more in the realm of work performance than pedigree and show performance, so she would have preferred to see this one work under a saddle.

But it was a complete pleasure to watch the big horse respond to signals and commands while she listened to Nick and Colby discuss the animal. The stallion's sleek coat shone in the sun, and his red hide moved over his powerful muscles like creek water over stones.

A female voice called out, interrupting Colby's long-winded talk and Corrie glanced over her shoulder to see a tall blonde walk toward them from the alley that bisected the corrals.

The woman carried herself as if she owned the world, and her blue, blue eyes were fixed on Nick as firmly as an arrow on a bull's-eye. Since the woman had to have noticed Corrie standing next to Nick at the fence, she must have already dismissed her presence.

"Hey there, Nick. Daddy said you were coming down today."

She walked straight to Nick, and Corrie stepped aside and stood by a little awkwardly as the woman took Nick's arm and prompted him to lean down for a kiss. But instead of a friendly peck on the cheek, her kiss landed full on his mouth in a way that looked too natural between them to have been the first time.

# CHAPTER NINE

WHY it looked that way to Corrie was more because there was no hint of shyness or hesitation in either the woman or Nick, and the fact that the kiss went on. And on. Corrie was stunned by the flash of anger that went through her.

Was this jealousy? She'd almost never felt more than a nettle or two of the roaring torment that scorched her now. She'd stood at the edge of a lot of things in life that she might have liked to have but knew she'd never get, and yet she'd never felt anything like this.

It was one thing to know she wasn't Nick's kind and that this woman was. It was another to see it demonstrated so starkly in close quarters. Though the woman wore a common yellow blouse and what looked to be a much more expensive brand of jeans than Corrie would ever buy, there was a sophistication about the way she carried herself that gave the impression of a fashion model who'd dressed down for the day.

Her sleek golden hair fell like bright silk to her shoulders, and her peaches and cream skin looked flawless. The elegant hand that had lifted to Nick's lean cheek had delicate, tapered fingers with manicured nails that would never survive a dishpan, much less a minute of outdoor work.

Though the kiss probably lasted a scant few seconds, Corrie lived those seconds in thousandths of time, and she felt untold relief when Nick straightened to end it. Corrie was careful to be caught watching the stallion instead of the kiss. She was glad Colby was standing more or less behind her left shoulder and couldn't see her face.

The beautiful blonde made a chiding sound and Corrie's gaze slipped back in time to see her reach up to whisk a smear of lipstick off Nick's lower lip, though it looked more as if she'd rubbed it in like a second kiss than rubbed it off. Corrie felt her heart fall a little more at the way Nick was smiling at the woman, so she looked away again.

"And who's this?" the woman said, finally turning to acknowledge Corrie, who warily looked over at her. "One of your people?"

Corrie felt the barb, but gave a calm smile. At least she hoped it looked calm. That "one of your people" crack was kinder than asking if Corrie was a stable hand, but she knew she'd just been put firmly under the blonde's boot. She also knew the blonde had to have noticed Nick's hand on the back of her waist moments ago so the question was a dig.

Corrie realized then that she'd handled situations like this in the past with men who'd given her similar little set-downs in work or business situations. Those were men who'd had a problem with a young female

rancher or a female doing men's work. The principle
was the same, and that was to ignore the snub and
politely assert herself.

Just as Colby started to introduce her, Corrie
stepped forward to put out her hand for a handshake.
The take-charge surprise of it made Colby's voice
stop midword and caused the blonde to reflexively
reach out before she'd had time to think about it.

"No, I'm just a neighbor," Corrie said with a smile
as she caught the blonde's hand. "Corrie Davis. And
you are?"

"Serena Blake," she answered then pulled out of
the handshake, her blue eyes darkening a little before
they flicked dismissively away from Corrie to Nick,
effectively cutting Corrie off before she could mur-
mur anything even remotely like "nice to meet you."

Which was just as well because it would have been
a lie. The feeling was obviously mutual, but that troubled Corrie. She was hardly a threat to the glamorous
blonde.

After that, Colby suggested they have a look at a
couple of mares stabled in a nearby barn that he
thought might interest Nick before they went back to
the pickup for the ride to the house. Corrie sat in the
back seat with Serena, who slid forward and draped
herself over the back of the front seat so she hung
between her father and Nick, chattering the whole
way about how Nick was buying her "baby" and
how much she'd miss the animal.

And of course wheedling for an invitation to visit

Merrick Ranch, which irritated Corrie to no end. She would never dream of doing something so shamelessly forward as inviting herself anywhere. Nick was left with no polite choice but to extend an invitation that sounded sincere, though it probably was. After all, this wasn't his first encounter with Serena Blake, not by a long shot.

Women as beautiful and obviously spoiled as Serena could flirt and wheedle and push any man to do whatever she wanted, even men as experienced and worldly-wise as Nick. She was also vivacious and glamorous and so completely female that Corrie couldn't imagine the man who could have resisted, worldly-wise or not, especially when she turned on the charm as she was now with Nick. But if Nick ever fell for a woman as presumptuous and manipulative as Serena Blake, Corrie would be hugely disappointed in him.

When they reached the house, Corrie got her handbag out of the car, then went along with the others into the massive single-story house to have lunch. They all washed up then met back in the living room before Colby offered his arm to Corrie to escort her into the dining room ahead of Nick and Serena.

The dining room, like the rest of the house, was grand and done in a kind of refined Southwestern decor that looked too professional to feel comfortable. Corrie was a little less awed by this house, but reckoned that was more because of Serena than anything else. Serena's father was jovial and gracious, and she'd liked that he wasn't as pretentious as his fine house and wealth might have made him. It seemed odd that Serena was so different.

Colby and Serena sat at opposite ends of the long table, leaving Nick and Corrie sitting across from each other in the center. Corrie looked over into Nick's gaze and felt a rush of pleasure at the twinkle in his dark eyes, as if the two of them shared some amusing secret.

It was a look that seemed to say, *Bear with this a little longer,* though that might be wishful thinking on her part. At least he seemed to be aware that she hadn't cared for Serena, and he appeared to have no quarrel with that, though Corrie hoped their host didn't realize how she felt. Nevertheless, she didn't intend to be anything less than polite to the woman and she sensed Nick understood that he could trust her to do that.

Colby was a talker who couldn't seem to tolerate uneven participation in a conversation. Corrie's tendency to listen more than speak was under friendly assault, and she decided she liked Colby, though he was a challenge to resist. He seemed interested in everything he could pry out of her, whether he really was or not.

Halfway through the meal, Corrie decided it was high time to go after Colby on something she'd like a big-time horse breeder like him to answer, particularly since it was something she was currently dealing with. At the very least, it might keep him talking long enough so she could finish eating.

"Have you ever had trouble keeping weight on a horse that's healthy otherwise?" she asked, and Colby was all too happy to not only tell her about the ones he'd had, but what he'd done about them.

That was enough to get her through to dessert. By then Colby had slowed down and Serena had taken over, though she kept the conversation mostly on herself or on Nick. After they finished dessert, then went into the den for coffee while the men conducted their business and arranged to transport the stallion to Merrick Ranch.

It was well after two by the time Colby and Serena walked them to the car. Colby invited Corrie to visit the Slash B anytime she liked, while Serena had a low-level conversation with Nick on the driver's side of the car. Corrie ignored the other two while she thanked Colby for his hospitality.

When they were finally on their way, Corrie felt relieved. She'd done well enough, and the challenge of being alone with Nick seemed far more manageable than dealing with either Serena or her friendly and talkative father.

"You charmed Colby," Nick remarked, and Corrie glanced over to see his faintly smiling profile. "And he was serious about that invitation to visit whenever you like."

"So you heard that," she said, secretly—and foolishly—pleased that he'd been listening, despite

Selena's effort to dominate his attention. "He was very gallant."

"He liked you. And I apologize for that kiss." Now his faint smile eased away. "There's some history there, but no future."

The statement sent a charge through her and she had to fight making too much of it.

"It's not really my business," she said, which made Nick glance over at her.

"You don't think so?"

Corrie felt her face color at the small challenge that seemed to hint at so much, but Nick chuckled then looked forward to watch the road. He didn't pursue an answer, and Corrie was glad of that. What could she have said anyway besides what they both knew was the truth? Nick's future or lack of a future with Serena Blake truly was none of her business, unless something wonderful happened and he made it so. She didn't want to even speculate on why he'd just seemed to hint it was.

It wasn't too much longer before she noticed a subtle tension between them, a tension that began to slowly draw tighter. All the way home, by car then plane then pickup, each glance, each smile, each lingering touch, everything—no matter how small or casual—suddenly seemed to be building toward something specific in a way it hadn't before.

By the time Nick at last turned off the highway onto the Davis Ranch drive, the pleasant on-again, off-again conversation between them had faded to silence. Though the talk between them had had its moments, it hadn't been filled with the kind of wit and brilliant verbal exchanges a man like him might prefer, and Corrie felt more than a little regret over that.

Nick had said going with him today might be a better way of getting acquainted, but she wondered how pleased he really was with the things he might have found out about her. She was still reserved with him, though less than before, and yet he'd been surprisingly open with her and a good companion. But the truth was, Nick had lots of other choices about the women he could spend time with, women who fit into his life in far more ways than she ever could.

At last her house came into sight and Corrie was suddenly impatient to be let out so she could change clothes and start chores. Anything to get back to normal, doing the things she was completely comfortable with, things that had nothing to do with whether she had a sparkling personality or not, or whether some man found her attractive.

Her brain was already calculating how many catch-up things she could get in tonight before bedtime, the more demanding and exhausting the better. Whatever it took to put today's outlandish wishes behind her as quickly as possible, though she'd never forget the day itself. The moment Nick pulled the pickup to a halt at the front walk, Corrie touched her seat belt release and gathered her things before she smiled over at him.

"I appreciate going along with you today. It was interesting and I enjoyed the company, but I hate to hold you up." She felt her smile falter a little because his gaze seemed to be searching hers a little too intently. "I need to start chores anyway."

The dark gaze that stared over into hers was pushing deeper as the seconds ticked by. She grew a little flustered, looked down briefly at the Stetson she was gripping so hard, and felt guilty for being so ungracious. "B-but if you'd like to come in for a while, I can get you an iced tea. Or make coffee." Now she made herself look over at him, hoping the offer made up for her lapse in manners. "It wouldn't take but a minute."

One side of his handsome mouth curved. "Let me give you a hand with the chores. I can take you to supper afterward." His low voice was quiet, and that gave her a quivery feeling inside.

She gave her head a doubtful shake. "You've put up with me enough for one day. And I can't let you do more, especially not chores on top of everything else. You aren't dressed for that anyway."

Nick chuckled and Corrie felt her racing heart leap when he reached over and took her hand.

"Are you scared to let me stay around and take you to supper?" Now his voice dropped to a gravelly rasp. "Or are you just shy because you know I'm going to kiss you?"

Corrie's gaze shot away from his and a frenzy of embarrassment and excitement stormed over her from head to toe, though terror was in the mix. She heard his seat belt release and her gaze flew back to his rugged face as he leaned toward her. His fingers were still gently gripping hers to keep her where she was as he reached up to tug off his Stetson. She swallowed hard when he dropped it to the floor and drew her toward him.

A last second quiver of excitement and dread almost made her turn her face before his mouth eased gently onto hers, but the surprisingly warm contact froze her for a moment and she hastily closed her eyes so he wouldn't catch her wide-eyed shock. But that next instant she forgot all about what anyone might see. At that first touch of his lips on hers, a small explosion of excitement had gone off in the deepest parts of her and the shards sparkled through every part of her body in delicious waves of sensation.

Corrie was lost so quick she didn't have time to think about whether she should close her lips or keep them open. The self-consciousness she'd felt with Shane's kiss the other night was completely absent now as a firestorm of breath-stealing heat began to roar through her.

Somehow she'd lifted a hand to Nick's lean cheek, unaware that she'd dropped her Stetson and handbag to do that. Nick slowly pulled her into his hard, strong arms as his gentle, probing kiss began to change into something far more demanding.

The kiss rapidly escalated into something that was barely civilized—or maybe *she* was barely civilized. All she knew was that this was the most wonderful feeling of her life and she was suddenly greedy for more, lots more, everything she could have. And yet her body felt oddly weak, though Nick's male strength seemed to easily compensate. If she'd had any sense left, she would have been mortified by the way she clutched at him and so quickly caught on to the things his lips and tongue were doing to hers.

The reserve of a lifetime had been cracked, then dispensed with so quickly and thoroughly that even if she'd had any sense of herself beyond pure physical sensation, she wouldn't have been able to get it back. Or have wanted to.

Instead, she wanted more of this. It was as if she'd waited her whole life for this kind of touching, this feeling of connection that was unlike anything she could have imagined before that moment. She was completely and utterly Nick's in those hot moments, and the rightness of it seemed to amplify every sensation until the kiss felt like a bond. Or a brand.

Just when Corrie didn't think she could survive the pleasure of it, the kiss began to slow, and the conflagration gradually began to die down. The unrushed kisses that followed were somehow even more potent and affecting.

At last they stopped and she tried to get her breath back. It was a shock to regain a sense of where they were, though that was a long time coming. And yet she felt an amazing sense of assurance and ease with Nick now, as if the wall of reserve he'd broken down would stay down and never come between them again. The rightness of that and her strong sense of connection to him was almost tangible.

And oh, his arms were so strong and warm and comforting. She never wanted to move away from his furnace-like heat or the solid feel of his hard chest.

"Will you let me hang around and help with chores?" he asked as he nuzzled her hair and pressed a kiss on her temple that sent new shivers of warm delight through her. He made her feel cherished, which made her emotional.

"Yes." Her whispered agreement was almost a reflex. That's when she detected the thread of worry in her heart. The worry that if she let him go home now, this wonderful thing between them—whatever it was and whatever it meant—might evaporate like a mirage and never come back.

"I still want to take you to supper afterward."

Her soft, "All right," was barely audible and Nick drew back to look into her flushed face.

"Something wrong?"

A bashful smile tried to burst out, and she barely had enough control of herself to be able suppress it, though her mouth trembled with the effort. "No...I can't really think of a thing that's wrong."

"Me neither," he said, then grinned. "Except I want more of that. But later, after the chores."

The bashful smile trembled a bit more out of her weak control, and Corrie made herself look away and pull back. It was stunningly hard to do that, but it was even harder to regain control of her foolish, foolish heart. It was soaring in the clouds with joy and unbounded hope.

And love. It was the most powerful feeling of love that she'd ever felt in her life, and it was Nick's, all Nick's. Her brain shied from the peril, because the feeling was too intense and wonderful to resist.

Nick went into the house with her and after she started coffee, Corrie raced upstairs to change and braid her hair. She was back down in record time, realizing the silliness of being so rabidly eager to see Nick again, but so caught up in the lingering magic and astonishment of this that she couldn't chance losing even a second of time with him.

# CHAPTER TEN

CORRIE felt as if she was walking about a foot off the ground. She could barely remember the order of her normal chore routine, and once they were done, she had to mentally review the list to be sure she hadn't left anything out.

Because Nick didn't want her to fuss with her clothes, they went to the Dairy Queen for hamburgers. The only thing he wanted her to do was unbraid her hair before they left, but he confessed the reason was because he wanted to do it for her.

"Your hair is so soft, like silk," he'd said as he'd combed his fingers through it as if he couldn't get enough of the feel. Then he'd used her brush on it. She'd had to brace her hand on the edge of the kitchen counter to keep from melting to the floor.

The experience had made her light-headed with pleasure. Then he'd turned her into his arms to kiss her, and performed the same sense-stealing magic he had earlier. Corrie was literally helpless to resist him, and she didn't have enough caution left to care about the danger of being so easily and completely captivated by him.

Corrie barely paid attention to what they ate later at the DQ, because what they ate couldn't possibly register on her like the wonder of being with Nick. On their way home later, she finally had to face the idea that the day was winding down and it would soon come to an end. She loved Nick so completely now that her heart shied fearfully from the knowledge. This was far more than a crush, and it had happened far too fast.

It took effort, but she finally convinced herself that she would let the day pass away when it did, however much she wanted it to go on. After all, she didn't realistically expect to have other days like this with Nick, but she'd at least had this one, and she refused to mourn either the end of it or to eat her heart out hoping for others if they never came. It would be a daunting task.

Nick drove around to the back of her house and walked in with her to the kitchen. She'd put their leftover coffee in a thermos and offered it to him now.

"We've still got coffee."

"None for me, thanks," he said as he caught her hand and pulled her into his arms. "I was wondering if you'd like to go dancing tomorrow night."

Corrie loved that the embrace felt so natural. "I've never danced," she said, untroubled now to admit something like that to Nick, who had more than proven both his acceptance and his respect. He grinned down at her.

"Well then, it'll be my pleasure to teach you. I'll come early to show you a few steps, but the one I'm most interested in is so simple you won't need a lesson.''

Then he leaned down and kissed her again, and just like the other times, her body responded as quickly to him as if he'd flipped a switch. Despite her earlier resolve to not mourn the close of this day, Corrie couldn't seem to lie to herself about the stark longing that gripped her when Nick gradually ended the kiss and told her good-night.

Once he was gone, she turned from the door and looked around the big kitchen. Nick's presence lingered, and somehow this old place felt warmer and less lonely. *She* felt warmer and less lonely, less separated from the things most other women her age took for granted. And at least for a while, a man wanted to spend time with her. Beauty, social position and money apparently didn't matter to Nick because she didn't have those. That a man like Nick seemed to be attracted to her anyway without all that was perhaps the most precious thing of all.

The novel feeling of being liked in the way Nick seemed to like her was a miracle, and she wondered now how she'd survived this long as an adult without knowing about exactly how it felt to have a man want her as a woman.

Corrie not only felt fully female, but fully feminine in ways she'd never known she could. There'd also been an odd little feeling of power when she'd felt the tremor in Nick's big body as his kisses had grown stronger and more carnal. It was as if he couldn't control his body's reaction to her, and yet she'd also felt him trying to hold back…but struggling, which was wonderful for her ego and made her reconsider her beliefs about herself.

*He wanted to take her dancing tomorrow night.*

She felt like dancing now. It took incredible self-will to make herself get some things done in the house and make a pass at paying a few bills. But after she'd taken her shower, she'd been unable to keep from going through her new clothes to decide what to wear tomorrow night.

She'd just made a decision when she heard the sound of a vehicle and walked into the hall to look out a window that faced the highway. It was Shane's pickup that drove into range of the yard lights so Corrie rushed back to her room to change out of her robe into fresh jeans and a T-shirt. She got downstairs in time to open the back door just as Shane came up the porch steps.

"Hey there, stranger," she said with a smile, then pushed open the screen door for him to catch before she stepped back into the kitchen. "I haven't seen you for a couple days."

Shane walked in, but the faint smile he gave her seemed a little forced. His blue eyes pierced hers and she felt her smile of welcome fade a little. He took off his Stetson.

"I'm sorry I didn't get back to you sooner," he said, and Corrie was struck by the remoteness in his manner.

"I've still got coffee in the thermos," she told him. "I could get you some and we could go sit in the living room."

"Nah, but thanks. I came by because I found out who the hombre was who riled you the other night. I wanted to give him enough time to make his apologies, but...I'm thinkin' now I might have given him a little too much time."

Corrie felt her cheeks go warm. "So Nick told you."

"Yup. And, for the record, he was genuinely sorry." Now one side of Shane's mouth kicked up and the somberness about him seemed to lift a little. "He took you to San Antonio today, huh?"

Corrie couldn't help noting the way he rotated the Stetson between his hands. "You don't...approve?"

"Sure I do."

"But?"

Shane's half smile eased a little. "But...just don't get too crazy too quick. That's all."

Corrie stared over at Shane. He'd put it in vague terms, but they'd been friends a lot of years. Too many years for her not to know what he was really saying.

She wasn't angry with Shane, but her heart was squeezing with hurt. Not because her friend was afraid she was headed for certain heartbreak, but because she knew he was right. She didn't really have a chance with Nick, not long-term. It was hard to keep that in mind when it had all felt so wonderful, so right.

She still wanted to believe it was right, at least for a little while. To have a day, or maybe a few days, to make up for lost time and maybe to dream a little. Maybe it was good that Shane had dropped by now, before this went further. Things did seem to be going too fast. Maybe it would be good to put the common sense reality of it into the words Shane would never say before she lost track of it again. Maybe it would be even better if she made herself listen to the words.

"I appreciate that you're enough of a friend to chance this," she began. Shane walked close and gently took her hand. Corrie made herself look him in the eye.

"But the truth is, you don't think your brother and I would be any kind of match, that I'm not the kind of woman who really has a chance with him. You'd never say it like that, but you're trying to warn me off before I make a fool of myself and get hurt."

The irony that Nick had warned her away from Shane years ago, only to have Shane warn her away from Nick now, however kindly Shane meant this, wasn't lost on her.

Shane's expression went grim. "You could never make a fool of yourself, Corrie," he said then tossed his Stetson to the table to take her other hand. "And my brother couldn't find a better woman than you."

She ignored his declaration and smiled up at him,

putting everything she had into it. After all, he knew her too well, so this had to be good.

"Oh, Mr. World Champion Bronc Rider," she said trying for a chiding tone as she gave his hands a little squeeze, "haven't you ever dallied with a woman you knew you'd never marry? Do you think you're the only person who's ever had a little affair with no mention or thought of marriage? Something you knew might not last a week, but felt too good to pass up?"

Shane's gaze was all but digging holes in hers and she almost couldn't keep that small, knowing smile on her face. Then she realized she was squeezing his fingers so hard that it was a wonder he didn't flinch.

"Oh, hell, honey," he rasped. In that next moment, Shane caught her against him, pressing her cheek against his chest while he kissed the top of her head then held her tighter.

Corrie squeezed her eyes closed, and snuggled against the warm comfort he offered. She should have known her little speech wouldn't succeed with him.

"Don't worry about me, Shane." She got the quiet words out and was proud that they sounded confident. "It's about time I grew up the rest of the way instead of hanging back. This really isn't a tragedy you know."

His arms tightened and she suddenly felt like bawling. She needed to lighten this up fast, so she tried to put a smile in her voice to go with the faked one she forced onto her mouth.

"And your brother's a fine kisser. I've learned a

couple things that might impress the next man who comes along.''

She pulled back a little then to look up at him. Shane's face was as hard as a brick, so she tried to chide him out of it. ''You're not so bad at it yourself, but you know that.''

Corrie almost thought he'd never smile, that he'd never let this moment pass. But then he let her have her way.

''A fine kisser, huh?'' he grumbled. ''I'm shocked at the way you're talkin', girl, but I get the message. Wish I didn't, but I do. I'll be going home now, but I'll be around. I'm also available whenever you need me, or want to talk.'' He gave her a hard, quick kiss on the cheek then glared down at her. ''You got that?''

Corrie tried to widen her faked smile, but she suddenly felt a wave of exhaustion like she'd rarely felt in her life, even after a brutally hard workday.

''I've got it,'' she said. ''Thanks. And thanks for not telling me how cheap I was to kiss you the other night then take up with your brother today. I didn't think you meant anything by that kiss the other night. You didn't, right?''

''Ha,'' he barked, then gave her a mock angry glare that was pure playacting. He was making a try at lightheartedness because he'd sensed she wanted him to, and she loved him for it. ''You cheated on me, woman. Toyed with my *manly* affections, then threw me over for an *older, richer* man.''

He let her go, then reached for his Stetson to put it on and tug it down in a teasing show of ire. "I've never seen the like," he went on, but winked. "You're a regular Jezebel in jeans, Corrie Davis. For shame."

Corrie laughed at that, though it was more from relief than amusement. "You'd better get on home. I need to get some sleep."

Shane smiled and reached over to gently chuck her under the chin. "Sleep tight then, baby. Lou will know where I am if you want to call. Just don't let me wait to hear from you. I might get the notion you don't love me no more." He made his smile turn down.

"I'll always love you, Shane." The truth of that made her choke up. Shane's voice went low and sounded almost as choked.

"Same with me, kid. G'night."

"G'night."

Shane left then and Corrie started through the house, turning off lights. When she got upstairs and undressed for bed, she slipped beneath the sheet and comforter but laid in the dark a long time, thinking, doing her best to put it all into a perspective that might insulate her from inevitable disappointment.

But it was like trying to clean up spilled syrup with a teaspoon. You could get some, but you needed to wipe it off the table with a wet dishrag so you could get it all and scrub away the sticky mess. She couldn't seem to bring herself to do that, not yet.

*     *     *

Nick came into the house just before noon that next day. The stallion had been delivered at midmorning, and he'd taken the rest of the time before lunch getting him settled in. He'd lost track of Shane, but they met up in the dining room. Shane had been silent and surly at breakfast and from the looks of it, his mood hadn't improved. Nick waited while Lou served lunch and hoped he could get through the meal before he found out the reason for Shane's bad mood.

He felt too good to let anything spoil it yet, and the reason he felt good was Corrie. Though the stallion had been a distraction, he hadn't been able to get Corrie off his mind. Not that he wanted to. He'd genuinely enjoyed being with her.

He'd enjoyed it so much that he hadn't wanted to leave last night. If she'd been like other women he'd dated, he might not have left so early, but it had been Corrie's innocence and her inexperience that had insured a chaste goodbye. She wasn't the kind of woman who would feel good about sleeping with a man she hadn't married first, so there was no sense putting her close to the possibility.

He accepted that and he approved. He'd come to agree with more traditional attitudes toward sex and intimacy himself. However great sex could be, it had always seemed to fall short of expectation. The outcome was always the same: physical satisfaction, but a feeling of emptiness afterward. Looking back, Nick wasn't sure if there'd ever been any real emotional satisfaction in it. A certain glow afterward maybe, and a level of tender feelings, but little more. Nothing worth pledging himself to.

From friends who'd been lucky enough to find a good woman, he'd come to understand that there was a big difference between a biological craving and the kind of sexual satisfaction and intimacy a marital relationship promised. The challenge of finding a relationship like that then keeping it exciting for the rest of his life, tantalized him. He'd committed his life to Merrick interests, faced the difficulties, enjoyed the rewards, and relished the steep challenge of keeping it all going.

Marriage seemed to be the same kind of mettle-testing challenge—more so because there were two people to satisfy and accommodate instead of just one—so he liked the idea of making a lifetime commitment to a wife.

Had the time come for him to marry? He'd gone his entire adult life without ever being tempted, but he suddenly couldn't think of anything else. He couldn't miss that it was because of Corrie Davis that he was thinking about it now, and his thoughts were stronger than he'd ever believed they'd be.

Despite her natural independence, Corrie knew the meaning of family, sacrifice and commitment in ways most women he'd known had no concept of. She'd sacrificed plenty because of her family commitment to a father who hadn't been worthy of it, so Nick took it for granted that she'd be even more devoted and committed to a husband who could genuinely be as devoted and committed to her in return.

Shane's grumbling voice prodded him out of his thoughts.

"I asked you a question, big brother. Twice. Are you just not speaking to me today or are you mooning over Corrie Davis?"

Nick heard the sarcasm in the question and the jealousy behind it, but he was caught a little off guard by the rush of possessiveness he felt toward Corrie.

And the almost primitive compulsion to stake some sort of public claim to her.

"You object to my interest in her." Nick stated it as a fact because Shane had made it crystal-clear. He gave his brother a level look that invited him to speak his piece. Shane seized the opportunity.

"Just what do you think you're doing with her? She's an innocent, Nick."

That nettled him. "You think I'm a despoiler of innocents?"

Shane put his fork down and rested his forearms on the table edge.

"I'm saying she's probably got about zero experience with boyfriends. And it's a fact that you might never have paid attention to her if you weren't so paranoid about me taking up with her and not staying around here to 'fulfill' my 'responsibilities'. Makes me wonder if you didn't start this just to keep her away from me."

Shane's accusation sliced deep, but Nick resisted the urge to slice back. "Do you want her?"

Shane's frown went darker. "I told you I didn't know yet, but it looks like you rushed right in before I could decide. And you damned sure got her to fall for you. I always wondered if she had a crush on you, and I figure now she must have. Probably didn't take her more than a second to lose her head, did it?"

Nick couldn't help the tickle of pleasure it gave him to know Corrie might have had a crush on him, but he couldn't show Shane that. It offended him that his brother didn't have more faith in him, but he was proud that Shane was taking up for Corrie. Because Nick approved of that, he decided not to retaliate for his brother's low estimation of his character.

"My intentions toward Corrie are honorable."

"Well good. Then you won't mind breaking it off with her now, before this goes on another day. You told me more than once that Corrie would never hold my interest and that I'd better keep my pants zipped. So I'm sayin' the same to you now. But if *you* foul up, you'll have a world of trouble and hurt on your hands. From *me,* and that's a promise."

Now Nick was riled. Shane was warning him off as if he was some randy kid instead of eight years his elder.

"You'd be welcome to try," Nick bit out and saw the flash of outrage in Shane's eyes as his expression hardened.

"Don't toy with her, Nick."

"Stay out of it, and mind your own business."

Shane grabbed his napkin from his lap and slapped it on the table. "Like hell I will."

Nick studied his brother's anger-flushed face and the rigid way he held himself. He probably looked just the same, but it was past time to defuse this. Shane was about an inch away from demanding they settle this outside, and Nick wasn't too far away from demanding it himself. He tried to keep his tone reasonable.

"I appreciate that you care for Corrie enough to want to protect her, but I honestly mean her no harm."

Shane searched his face in those next tense seconds before his rising anger seemed to level off a little, then marginally deflate. Nick got the impression that Shane regretted this, at least some of it. But then Shane seemed to cool off a little more and expelled a terse breath.

"Ah, hell, Nick," he said, then fidgeted with his discarded fork, as if he had to drag out what he said next. "I know you wouldn't mean to hurt her—"

"Well thanks for that much."

Shane had the grace to look a little chastened, and made an effort to mellow more of his temper. "But what I'm saying is—"

"What you're saying is, you're in love with her."

Nick's statement set off a shockwave of silence that he let go on only a few moments before he spoke again. "But you *might* be able to take it if she fell for someone else. As long as that someone else made her happy.''

Shane took in a quick breath to shoot back, but then exhaled again and glanced away. "Well, you nailed it, Sherlock. The minute I saw her again, it smacked me right in the chest, so I can't blame you if it happened to you too.''

Now his blue gaze came back to Nick's and burned angry again, though not as strongly. "It *ought* to have happened to you. If it hasn't yet, then I hope you'll step back.''

Nick gave him a measuring look. "If I don't love her like you do *yet*, and if I don't step back, what then? Would she come between us as brothers?''

"She already has, bro," Shane pointed out before the sarcastic slant of his mouth faded to earnestness. "But I don't want her to come between us.''

Nick was mollified by that. "I don't want her to come between us either. There are at least a million potential girlfriends and wives in this world, but you and I only have one brother apiece.''

Nick waited for that to sink in, waited until he saw the last of the angry aggression in his brother mellow more before he went on.

"I'm not sure I want to risk the only brother I'll ever have. We've had enough bumpy times, and maybe more to come. But if all it takes to smooth that out is to leave the way open for you and Corrie, then I'd feel compelled to consider stepping back.''

Shane's gaze narrowed on him as he seemed to

think about that. "What are you offering? To let me have Corrie if I'll stay on and be a full partner here?"

Nick gave his head a firm shake. "I didn't say that, but I might consider it. In exchange, there'd be a fifty-fifty split in ownership and authority. We'd have to take care of whatever legalities are involved to make it that, but yes, I'd consider it if you came into equal partnership with me."

"Would you want that kind of deal?"

"I want my brother at my side, here on Merrick, where we both belong. I've always wanted that. If you and I can peaceably work things out over a woman we both want, then there wouldn't ever be anything too difficult to negotiate and reach an agreement on in the future."

Shane eyed him a moment, but his skepticism was blatant. "You could do that?" Nick's gaze slid away.

"I didn't say it would be a cakewalk. But like you said, it's better to back off now if that's the way it has to be."

"Oh, sure." Shane chuckled grimly. "I can see the three of us living together under this roof, sitting together at this table, sleeping down the hall from one another."

Nick's gaze came back to his as Shane went on. "And how cold-blooded are you to even suggest using Corrie as a bribe to get me to stay on here? That can only mean that you *are* using her. Damn it, Nick, I can't begin to tell you how low down that is."

Nick only barely ignored the accusation and played

this out. "Would you rather have Corrie and stay on with me, or would you'd rather stay completely independent of family responsibility? And her."

Shane stared at him a long time, his blue eyes blazing again with a conflagration of anger and resentment. Nick could see it the moment Shane began to understand what was going on. Then Shane's mouth slanted again.

"You're testing me, aren't you? Offer me Corrie in exchange for my promise to stay on and take over my half of Merrick. See if I love her more than I love my plans to get my own place."

Nick let a hint of his approval show. "You've been demanding that I make a final decision about Corrie before I'm sure of what it will be. It might teach you a little something if you thought about facing the same instant demand, with roughly the same level of risk and reward at stake."

Shane laughed at that and it was a good sound. "You just can't help it, can you? Always the big brother. If you're not makin' me dig fence post holes in a drought, you're givin' me a taste of my own medicine." He chuckled again and gave Nick a warm glance. "I do appreciate the lessons though, cause I know how you mean them."

But then a competitive gleam came into Shane's eyes and a faint smile curved his mouth.

"What if I kept my plans and wooed Corrie away from you anyway?"

Nick shrugged. "You're welcome to do what you

want, since you're your own man. Meanwhile, I'll be doing what I want. Anything beyond that is up to Miss Davis. She's just as free to do as she pleases and to choose for herself as we are.''

Shane leaned back then and his smile widened. ''All right, big brother, the lady can choose between us. But the warning still goes: hurt her and you get pounded.''

Satisfied by that, Nick gave a nod and they both got back to their meal.

# CHAPTER ELEVEN

SLEEP had been too long in coming last night for Corrie, and the day was crammed with work that just couldn't wait. The effort was made harder by her lack of appetite and her inability to force down a big enough breakfast to keep her energy up until lunch. Then she hadn't made it back to the house until after one.

She should have checked cattle yesterday, but now it was too hot to go out alone on horseback, so she had to at least drive through the pastures during the hot part of the afternoon and pray none of her cattle needed doctoring. She routinely kept on top of that, so there shouldn't be a problem.

And there was a fence she needed to check along with a couple of stock tanks. She'd be more careful with her free time in the future. Taking most of a day to go shopping in town, then going away for most of another with Nick had put her too far behind. It shocked her a little to realize how irresponsible that was in the face of the amount of work to be done. She wouldn't do it again.

She wouldn't go dancing with Nick tonight either. The decision had taken a while to get to, and maybe part of the reason she'd pushed herself so hard that morning was to ensure she'd be too tired to do anything that evening but go to bed.

She was chancing real hurt with Nick anyway and she hadn't needed to have Shane come by last night to caution her about it. The truth was, she was worried she might be "easy". The old euphemism for a woman who'd go to bed with any man who wanted to, suddenly seemed to describe her a little too closely.

Not that she'd give herself to just any man, but she might to Nick. Her feelings for him were so deep and her reaction to him last night had been so strong that Nick could have had her in a New York minute. Or just about any other time he decided to. The idea worried her because she'd always thought if she ever did fall for someone, she'd never be seriously tempted to do anything counter to her beliefs.

But she felt helpless against Nick. He could also break her heart afterward in about half that New York minute, so what would she be left with? For her, the lonely outcome would be made worse by disappointment in herself for being so foolish. As miserable as it would be to distance herself from Nick now, the misery could be even worse if she waited for him to lose interest.

And what if his interest in her was at least partly because of Shane? Until the brothers resolved their dispute over inheritance and Shane's separate plans, she'd never really be sure how much of that was responsible for Nick's attention.

She'd been in love with Nick for years but the love she felt for him now made her too vulnerable. She didn't dare let herself do something she'd regret, especially if there was even a slim chance that Nick wasn't entirely sincere on any score, and she simply couldn't trust herself to resist the temptations he presented.

Maybe it was because this was so new. Nick had been in control of himself last night, but he was also more experienced. On the other hand, she wasn't certain any amount of experience would help her. Not when her heart was so involved.

It was just best all the way around to slow things down. It might be good anyway to avoid giving Nick the idea that she was always available to him. She'd already shirked enough work to be with him, so she had to be sensible from here on. Even though slowing things down might make him lose interest sooner, it might be for the best.

If Nick was going to lose interest anyway, pride dictated she cut things off before he could. His ego wouldn't suffer so much as a scratch, since he had plenty of women who were attracted to him, including the beautiful Serena. Her ego was a lot more fragile, so she had to protect it, however selfish that was.

It was hard to scrape up the courage to make the call to cancel Nick's plans, but once she'd had something to eat and had a ten-minute nap, she phoned Merrick Ranch and asked for Nick. He wasn't available, so it was a cowardly relief to leave her message with Miss Louise.

After that, she went back out to check cattle. Except for chores, she'd probably be away from the house until near dark this time, so she wouldn't be around for a return phone call that might tempt her to go dancing tonight.

The Davis Ranch house was mostly dark except for the series of yard lights around the modest headquarters. When Nick pulled around to the back, he felt a shaft of irritation. Shane's pickup was parked under the yard light that lit most of the house and the space between it and the nearest barn. He immediately wondered if Corrie had canceled their date tonight because of Shane. He pulled in beside the other truck and saw his brother perched on the porch rail, with no sign of Corrie.

As Nick got out of his truck and walked to the porch, he saw two pizza boxes balanced on the rail along with a six-pack of soda beside them.

"Hey there, big brother. So Corrie's not over home with you, huh?" There was nothing angry in Shane's tone, but there was a suspicious friendliness in it that gave a hint of rivalry.

"Pizza gone cold?" Nick asked as he briefly turned to glance toward the barns. He couldn't locate Corrie's pickup, though that depended on where she'd parked it, so he looked back to Shane.

"Yup. Sodas gone warm, too," Shane said. "Maybe she's out with someone else."

Nick stepped up onto the porch and reached to open the screen door. "Did you knock?" he asked, then did it himself.

"Her truck's not here, so no sense knocking. She didn't answer my phone call earlier tonight either, so she's been out most of the evening. I expect she won't be too much longer, since everyone gets up early around here." Shane grinned. "No reason for you to hang around too. I'll tell her you were by, and give you a full report when I get home. Or in the morning, since you take early nights too."

"Watch yourself, Romeo," Nick bantered back in the same competitive vein as he let the screen door close. "If you get your own place, there won't be so many late nights for you either, so you might want to start getting back in the habit tonight. When Corrie gets home, I'll let her know you were by. I'll pass on any message she might have for you at breakfast."

Shane chuckled. "This is payback, isn't it, for all those times I hung around you when you were trying to entertain a lady?"

Nick shook his head. "Nope. I'll pay you back for those when you give up trying to steal my woman and find one of your own."

"Is that right? Huh."

Nick found a perch for himself on the other porch rail. He saw a small flash of light coming from a pasture off to the west that he didn't think Shane had seen. He saw it again and then a pair of headlights came over the rise in the distance.

"Does Corrie work this late?" he asked Shane, then nodded in the direction of the headlights.

Shane looked over at them a moment, then remarked, "Not that I know of, but maybe you tied up too much of her time yesterday so she had extra today. She probably trades off work with a couple of other small operations and hires a couple part-timers like her daddy used to. I think she works alone more often than not."

"Her daddy also had her to help him," Nick commented, feeling guilty over Shane's remark about him tying up too much of Corrie's time yesterday.

"Yeah. A kid shouldn't have had to work like she did." Now Shane glanced his way and grinned. "I'll let her know you were here if you'd like to get on home."

Nick smiled faintly but didn't comment. Now they could hear the pickup engine as it shifted direction to drive to one of the main gates. They watched as Corrie got out and opened the gate, got back in the truck to drive through, then got out again to close it. It was only a couple more moments before she drove onto one of the lanes then turned a last time to drive to the main barn and park the truck near the door.

Shane slid off the rail to walk to meet her, but Nick stayed where he was. Though her Stetson shaded her face, Corrie looked neither surprised nor pleased that they were here, and Nick sensed right away that she wouldn't like this. Because he did, he wished now that he'd left her to Shane and his pizzas. The least he could do was not to directly compete with Shane.

After all, he had at least some confidence in Corrie's feelings for him, so he shouldn't have allowed Shane to draw him into even this much competition. Corrie was too reserved to appreciate that, though he knew plenty of women who would have loved it.

He noted she didn't say much to Shane when he met her, then fell into step at her side for the walk to the house. Shane didn't act as if that was anything different than usual, but Nick suspected it might be.

He heard Shane ask, "How come you're out so late?" but Corrie's reply had been too low to hear before Shane went on. "I brought pizza. Triple pepperoni, double mozzarella, and about a dozen packs each of those dried Eye-talian peppers and that sprinkle cheese you like. We'll have to heat 'em up now though."

Corrie took off her Stetson as she reached the porch steps. Her quiet, "Hello, Nick," was stiff, as was her nod of acknowledgment. "I reckon we might as well get inside. Now that I see you're both here, I think I've figured out something."

With that, she led the way into the house, hung her Stetson on a wall peg and walked to the hall door.

"Go ahead and heat the pizza," she called back before she stepped out of sight. "I need to wash up."

A door closed down the hall and Nick heard the sound of running water.

Meanwhile, Shane seemed to know his way around her kitchen. In moments he'd washed up, found pizza pans in a lower cupboard, switched the pizzas out of the box onto them, then slid the first pan into the oven before he set both the temperature dial and the timer. This wasn't the first time Shane had done such a thing, and Nick suspected his brother was more than happy to demonstrate that.

Nick hung his hat on one of the wall pegs, but noted that Shane had upended his on a counter. Meanwhile, the water was still running down the hall. He might not have appreciated walking in this late to company himself, but maybe Corrie would be glad for a meal she hadn't needed to cook for herself.

*Now that I see you're both here, I think I've figured out something.* Nick couldn't miss the idea that she'd meant exactly that and would have something to say about it. Since it made sense that Shane might have seen her sometime since last night or to at least have talked to her on the phone, Corrie might have some idea about Shane's determination to compete for her.

The water stopped running down the hall and after a few moments, Nick heard the door open. When Corrie walked into the kitchen, she smiled at Shane.

"Thanks for bringing pizza. It already smells good."

"I hope you still like triple pepperoni."

"I haven't had pizza for a long time. Thanks

again.'' Now she glanced over at Nick. "The two of you might as well sit down.''

Shane spoke up. "No, you two sit. I'll get the sodas iced and play waiter. Shouldn't be long.''

Corrie smiled, uneasy about this, but there was nothing polite to do but try to deal with it. She'd thought about Nick all day and then Shane that afternoon, particularly about Shane's kiss the other night and his manner with her last night. She now believed he'd been upset that she'd taken up with Nick, however much he'd tried to make a joke of it.

Though she was weary, Corrie had realized the moment she'd seen them both on the porch what might be going on. And there was something about Shane tonight too, something a little daring, something that seemed aimed at Nick, who was mostly silent and remote. It was a cinch the pizza hadn't been a joint project between the brothers.

Corrie sat at her usual place at the table and leaned back, relieved the day was coming to an end. She was careful to keep from looking either Nick's way or Shane's more than once, though that single glance at each man's somber expression emphasized her sense that they were at odds.

What she really wanted to do was go straight to bed. A wearying kind of fatigue that was no doubt a combination of hard work and lack of appetite didn't help, but dread of what she sensed between the Merrick brothers was also weighing on her. She ached. Not from the hard day, but because if she was right about her impression, her strong statements about it later were sure to alienate them both.

Shane set the sodas on the table and gave her an extra can, before he put out the plates and pizza slicer, then turned back to the oven when the timer began to buzz. He got the pizza on the table and resliced two thick wedges before he shifted them to her plate and passed the slicer to Nick.

"You can help yourself, big brother. I forgot the napkins."

Despite her lack of appetite that day, the moment Corrie sprinkled the dried peppers and parmesan on her pizza and had a first bite, she was suddenly ravenous. Her body could only take so much hard work without good food, and the hot pizza was a treat she only rarely indulged in.

Shane rejoined them at the table and served himself. Corrie was content to stuff herself while Shane and Nick exchanged a few trivial bids for conversation, only allowing herself to be briefly drawn into it twice. She felt both men watching her a lot of the time, but it was Nick's gaze she coveted. Though Shane was here and tension was high between the three of them, she felt a keener connection to Nick. It might not last the night though, and she silently grappled with that until they'd finished eating.

Conversation had become a chore for both brothers several minutes ago and a somber stillness had settled on the room, so Corrie tried to collect her thoughts.

She felt better now after the hot food, and again thanked Shane for bringing it.

"It really hit the spot," she said and smiled over at him. "I feel a little bad, though, that I ate your pizza just before I maybe rile you. I hope you know I don't mean to do that." She looked over at Nick. "I don't mean to rile you either, but I'm afraid something's going on between the three of us that I don't want."

The tension between them shot up a good foot as she toyed with her glass of soda. The silence now was unbelievably intimidating, but she managed to gather her courage. She kept her gaze on the glass as she began.

"Have the two of you worked out your differences over Merrick interests versus Shane's plan to get his own place? Or are you still at a standoff?"

That said, she looked up, first at Nick, then at Shane. It took a lot to do that and project any kind of calm, though she did it. Both men's expressions hardened, and she saw the light of battle come into Shane's gaze, and figured the answer was no.

"I'm going to guess at a few things," she announced quietly. "Right or wrong, I want to get them said. You can agree or disagree some other time, because I need some sleep."

She looked over at Nick and spoke bluntly.

"I think you've used guilt to get Shane to stay, because you feel guilty. Maybe because what the two of you inherited wasn't equal, and maybe your daddy favored you. I'd feel guilty over that if it was me. And yet you're bound to be disappointed in Shane because your life is full of duty and obligation that you think should be half his. He's consistently avoided it, maybe even outright refused it. And you can't understand why he'd want to build something of his own when you both own Merrick, so his plans seem foolish and irresponsible to you.''

She'd tried not to let her eyes focus too clearly on Nick's stony expression, so it was at least a relief to look over at Shane. She appreciated that Nick hadn't tried to argue.

"And Shane, you still haven't gotten over growing up with two bosses, so now you don't want any. You don't want to be the kid brother anymore, but Nick's the only brother you'll ever have. Do you understand how guilty Nick might feel? Maybe he missed being just your brother after your dad was hurt and he had to run everything and be responsible for you. And you Merricks have a lot in life, but you don't seem grateful. You don't seem to respect what a generous and honorable thing it is for Nick to want you to, as you said, 'rule and reign' with him.''

Blue fire came into Shane's gaze and she knew she was close to losing him. She'd been planning to shift the pressure back onto Nick, so she hoped what she'd say to him next wouldn't sound as if she'd been influenced by Shane's silent anger just now.

"And do you, Nick, understand how much Shane is like you? His dream is different than the one you expect him to love and commit to. I'm not sure I completely understand why the solution to your dispute has to be an either/or thing, because that doesn't seem reasonable. He's the only brother you'll ever have too, and it's a pure shame you don't seem interested in a middle road. Maybe you are, but does Shane know it?''

Now she divided her gaze between both brothers. ''You two are lucky. Pardon me for putting it this way, but you're *damned* lucky to have each other. I'd have given just about anything to have a brother or sister. I like to think I could work out a similar problem, but maybe I couldn't either. I'll never have to though, and there's not a single person in my life I have to consider other than myself, so I can afford to be selfish because no one will get hurt or be bitter.''

Now she pushed back her chair and stood. ''Seeing you both here tonight makes me think I've been a distraction. Since you don't seem to have worked out your differences, then I can't be sure I can trust the reason that might be behind any of the things that have gone on the past few days. From *either* of you. No offense, but I think you're both using me to avoid an outright showdown. Or maybe even to manipulate each other. I don't know, and that's for you to decide, so I don't want either of you to come around anymore unless I hear you've worked out your troubles without hard feelings or a feud.''

Shane spoke up first. ''Corrie, hon—''

''If I'm wrong about this, I'm wrong,'' she cut in,

gripping the back of her chair as she stared down at the table to avoid looking at either brother. "That doesn't change the fact that I don't want to see or hear from the two of you until I'm sure I'm not still in the middle. And I've talked more tonight than I wanted to as it is. Now I need some sleep. Good night to you both."

Corrie was grateful when she heard both of their chairs scrape back. She still couldn't look at either brother, but felt compelled to stop Shane when she saw him move to clear the table. "Thanks anyway, but I'll get the table. Next time the pizza's on me."

It was at least some consolation that neither of them said a word other than a mumbled version of good night before they both went out the door. Corrie cleared the table as she heard the truck engines start up, then drive around to the front drive and the high-way.

She must have been mostly right about the brothers. *Both* brothers. She hadn't said in so many words that she thought Nick might be using her to keep her from influencing Shane, not only because she wasn't certain about that but because she didn't want it to be true. Though Nick had invited her over the other night to surprise Shane, he'd at least con-fessed later that he'd had other motives, which he'd apologized for.

Corrie did have faith in his sense of honor, but just because he was a man who seemed to know his mind didn't mean he was completely aware of his every motive at every moment. Whether he'd set out to lure her away from Shane or he'd honestly noticed there was something about her that he was attracted to, Nick needed to clear things up with Shane. She was a distant second to that goal for both Merricks.

Taking herself out of the mix not only eliminated the possibility that she was being used, but stopped things with Nick before her heart was put in even more peril. She'd take what satisfaction she could in that, though it felt mighty puny now.

After she switched off the lights, went upstairs and got her shower, Corrie fell into bed. That night she immediately went to sleep.

# CHAPTER TWELVE

DURING those next days Corrie pretended it was easy to forget that Shane had come home, or that she'd spent a little time with Nick.

But then she'd remember the feel of Nick's arms around her and his lips on hers, and she'd recall every second, every look, and every word between them. She couldn't brush her hair now without thinking about how it had felt when Nick had brushed it. And just the sight of the indigo outfit she'd laundered and hung in her closet brought back memories from that day. She'd finally taken the jeans and shirt to hang them in another upstairs closet.

She couldn't do chores without remembering Nick doing those with her either, and it hadn't taken too long before she realized he'd somehow imprinted himself in far too many of the places she had to be every day. It would take some doing to banish his memory from those too.

Corrie had thrown herself into work that first two days. Then she'd gone to church on Sunday morning, and she'd worn one of the dresses she'd bought during her shopping spree with Eadie. Eadie had also been at church, so they'd sat together and afterward Corrie had invited Eadie to lunch. She'd put a roast in the oven earlier, and there'd been more than enough for company.

Corrie also filled her friend in on the things that had happened since the morning she'd come over to help with makeup, though she'd glossed over the details. Eadie seemed to think Nick would be back, but Corrie couldn't let herself hope too much for that.

Both brothers appeared to have taken her wishes seriously, because she hadn't heard a word from them, nor had she caught so much as a glimpse of either Nick or Shane in Coulter City the few times she'd been in town. She hadn't got on the wrong side of Shane's temper since eighth grade, and Nick had no real investment in continuing a relationship with her, so she might have lost both a long friendship and a fleeting romantic attraction in the same night. It was hard not to feel low about that.

To her utter surprise that next week, Corrie got a call from the son of another local rancher, one of her few former classmates who was still unmarried. He'd spoken to her at church on Sunday, but he'd called to ask her out to supper and a show. Since she'd survived her day-long semidate with Nick, she'd seen no reason not to accept the invitation.

Dane had been a pleasant date, one she'd been surprisingly comfortable with. She'd tried the cosmetics again, worn another of the dresses she'd bought, and felt a major rise in confidence by the end of a nice evening that had gone well. It was a relief when Dane saw her to her door but didn't kiss her good night, though he did ask if he could call her to go out again soon.

After that first two weeks, Corrie eventually decided she wasn't doing too badly without the Merrick brothers. If nothing else, that handful of days had changed some of her beliefs about herself and caused her to try a few new things that were already proving a benefit.

Life would move on even more before too long, and eventually this low feeling would fade completely away.

Late one afternoon Corrie came into the house, saw the blinking light on her answering machine, and pressed the button to play it. The message was brief.

"We've got some unfinished business, Miss Davis. I'll come by to settle up about seven tonight."

The moment she'd heard Nick's gravelly voice, her heart squeezed with an excitement and relief that made it impossible to keep her expectations modest, though she was compelled to. After all, Nick's low voice had sounded tough and grim. Rather than the miracle her foolish heart was clambering for, he might instead plan to give her a choice piece of his mind for the things she'd said the last time she'd seen him. Maybe things had gotten worse between him and Shane because of her. The idea spoiled any reason to feel optimistic.

But the next message that played was from Shane.

"If you're still speakin' to me, I'd like to stop by around eight. Give Louise a call if I'm not welcome."

Corrie instantly teared up, surprised at the powerful feelings that surged through her. She'd been afraid she'd lost Shane, and it was only after hearing his voice now that she let herself face how terrible it would have been to have lost his friendship forever.

She rewound the tape on the ancient machine and listened to both messages again, felt the same relief and excitement, but also had the same worries about what Nick had meant by his message. From Shane's, she'd got the impression that he was still her friend, but...what was Nick now?

The unfinished business he'd referred to could mean more than one thing and, considering how truly unattainable he was on a permanent basis, Corrie didn't dare take it to mean that he wanted to take up where they'd left off.

And he'd said they'd "settle up". No doubt Nick was ready to refute the things she'd accused him of in front of Shane that night, which had now been almost three weeks ago. Nick's stern tone seemed to indicate that was more likely than not.

And yet, it was odd that he'd set a time. Why would he do that if he'd decided to confront her about the things she'd said? Why not just show up and deal her the extra upset of a sudden, unexpected confrontation? Or was it more awful to know he was coming and worry? For her, it was more awful to have time to worry about it, so maybe Nick had figured that out.

But to have both brothers call on the same day to state plans to see her on the same night must mean they'd at least settled things between them. She'd made it clear she didn't want contact with either of them unless they had, and since she'd pretty much avoided people who would know the latest news in the area, she'd heard nothing about either of the Merricks.

Corrie didn't know if Shane had bought a place and would go off on his own, or if he'd given in and committed himself to Merrick interests. Could he and Nick have come up with a compromise? The only thing she was sure of was that she'd be having company tonight.

And since she wouldn't dream of calling either brother back and telling them not to come, she raced through the house to straighten up the little that needed straightening, then dashed outside to get her chores done. It seemed to take forever to finish then rush back to the house for a bite to eat and a quick shower and change of clothes.

The indigo blouse went well with her white jeans, though she'd almost talked herself into plain jeans and a work shirt at least half a dozen times. She hadn't rebraided her hair after she'd washed and dried it because she'd already guessed that if Nick had truly liked it as much as he'd claimed, wearing it loose might give her an advantage if he was coming over to talk to her as toughly as he had six years ago. But then, slim hope always grabbed for slim chance.

Though it didn't seem possible after the time they'd spent together that Nick would ever be harsh with her, it was foolish to think he couldn't be. Her insides were so tied in knots dreading it that she paced the house before she went to the kitchen to start coffee. She thought about the Dutch apple pie she'd baked that morning, and wondered if there'd be a chance to serve it to the brothers after Shane got here. Since she had it on hand, it might make a nice peace offering.

Corrie made a last trip to the bathroom mirror to check her makeup and hair, then heard the sound of a pickup engine. She rushed out, saw that it was five till seven, then blurted a hasty, desperate prayer as she heard the pickup drive around to the back. The engine cut and her heart began to pound.

*Friends always came around to the back.* Corrie tried to convince herself that she and Nick were still at least that, but then she heard his heavy bootsteps on the porch stairs and the all-business sound as he crossed to the door and knocked. At least she'd waited until he'd knocked this time, and she made herself walk at a normal pace to the door and open it.

Nick was so big and tough-looking. The moment his gaze connected with hers, she felt the punch of it. He reached up and swept off his Stetson. His manner was coolly formal.

"Miss Davis? I appreciate you seeing me tonight."

Corrie was choking on both excitement and dread. He was dressed in another stark white shirt with a turquoise bolo tie. He was wearing black dress pants and his black boots were polished to a high luster. He looked a good ten feet tall and about as muscular as a giant.

But his aftershave was the same faint, musky one she'd liked the day they'd flown to San Antonio, so realizing that made her relax the tiniest bit since she associated it with his kisses in particular. Surely he wouldn't come over dressed so nicely and wearing aftershave if all he meant to do was give her what-for.

Corrie managed a slight smile and stepped back. "Please, come in," she said, hiding her dismay over her breathless voice. That's when she realized she was shaking and instinctively started to hide her hands before she made herself stop the action. Her voice was no stronger when she got out a choked, "Would you like to go into the other room?"

Nick smiled a little then, and it magically altered his rocky expression. He hung his black Stetson on the wall peg next to hers. "It's a nice evening," he said. "The porch swing out back might be nice too."

Corrie felt heat surge into her cheeks and her gaze skittered from his. She knew now that this wasn't about a dispute, and that there'd be no hard words. But the words she sensed might be coming had to be the product of wishful thinking and feminine whimsy rather than anything realistic.

"Wherever you like is fine," she said.

Nick turned to push open the screen door for her

to precede him. Corrie stepped out then walked to the far end of the porch to the swing as he followed. She turned over the all-weather cushion so the good side was up, then sat down.

Nick sat down next to her, and she felt her heart quiver with delight when his fingers closed around hers and he gave her hand a gentle squeeze. At least that felt natural. And reassuring.

"Shane's offered for a place he likes," Nick began without preamble. "He's going it alone. His percentage stays the way it is for the next five years, and he'll compensate me out of his share of Merrick profits for handling Merrick responsibilities. If the market holds and he still wants to stay in business for himself, then I'll start buying some of his percentage until he's left with twenty-five percent, which will eventually pass to his heirs. Did you know he's thinking about going into business as a stock contractor?"

Corrie gave her head a small shake. "I didn't know that. We didn't talk about it though." She looked at Nick then, loving the warm light in his dark eyes. "Are you happy with that arrangement?"

"It wasn't what I hoped for, but I'm happy it's what he wanted. And he's probably right. You can't put two bulls in a single pen without asking for trouble. The fight's over, no hard feelings," he said, and Corrie was relieved.

She glanced away for a few moments because it made her ache to look at him, and she was afraid he'd see how hopelessly in love she was with him. Thankfully, he didn't seem to notice and went on.

"There came a time when I was fighting myself more than him. I did feel guilty like you said, but in some ways, I was also jealous. Merrick was handed to me. I'll never know what it's like to start small and build up to something substantial, and I envy him for that." He chuckled. "Shane'll have the time of his life, if it doesn't kill him."

Corrie looked at Nick, pleased that things had resolved in the way they seemed to have. "I'm glad," she said. "And relieved. I worried that I'd made things worse."

"You're pretty savvy about Shane and me," he said, and she felt her face heat again and looked down at their hands. "And I love when you blush like that. Makes me feel like the sexiest man in Texas."

A little giggle slipped out and Corrie sent him a chiding look. "You say such...extravagant things."

"I feel extravagant when I look at you. And right now I feel like I've got about five seconds to convince you to let me kiss you before I lose control and have to steal a kiss. May I?"

Corrie had to force herself to look him in the eye, because the infernal bashfulness that came over her seemed so childish. But there was nothing childish about the things Nick was saying. Or the deep, deep craving to have him kiss her again.

"You may."

Corrie managed to keep her gaze locked with his

as he leaned close. His lips settled tenderly on hers and her lashes fell shut. The kiss lasted a mere scattering of heartbeats before he drew her fully into his arms. Then the kiss deepened and became so carnal that the world heated up and spun. By the time it ended, Corrie was sitting across Nick's lap. She was so weak that she rested her hot forehead against his neck and tried to get her breath back.

Nick's gravelly voice was low and raspy. "It's months too soon, but I've never been one to dawdle or wait around once I make up my mind. So I brought you something."

Corrie's heart gave a leap and she lifted her head to look into his face. A half smile that played around his handsome mouth and the glitter in his dark eyes sent a flurry of happy sparks through her.

She barely got out the words, "What did you bring?" before he moved his hand from her hip and lifted it to dig in the shirt pocket that was between her breast and his skin. The casualness of that touch had anything but a casual effect on her and Corrie felt the heat of it arrow deep.

Nick held up what he'd taken out of his pocket and waited for her to look at it. When she did, she saw a large diamond on a smooth gold band encircling the tip of his index finger. Though he'd given her enough of a hint to know this was coming, the actual sight of the beautiful engagement ring was a profound shock. And the stone was large—huge!

"It's…big." The idiotic words made her gaze flash

up to his, half in fear that he'd think she was a ninny, but a slow smile was spreading across his mouth.

"You bet it's big, darlin'," he growled. "I've got big plans. Plans to marry, plans to have a good marriage with the woman I'm in love with at my side. And kids. I hope you want at least a couple, and I'm not particular about boys or girls, though I'd like to have at least one of each. How about you?"

"I don't have much family to speak of. I always wanted one though. Big, if I could."

"You can with me, Corrie. Is there any chance you might come to love an hombre like me?"

She couldn't have anticipated the question if she'd had a hundred years to think it up, and it touched her. There was a faint hint of uncertainty in it, which stunned her. A man like Nick Merrick shouldn't ever wonder whether a woman could love him or not, particularly not her. The idea that he wondered anyway was amazing. It was also something she had to answer right away.

"Oh, Nick. I've loved you since I was seventeen," she said, her voice that dismaying cross between a squeak and a whisper. "You really feel...the same?"

"I love you, Corina Jean Davis. I saw you watering your flowers and I felt it then, though I wouldn't have called it love. But then you came to supper and got hold of my heart. When you walked away that night because I'd not been honest with you, I knew by the way I felt that I'd just found the right lady. Will you come live with me and be my wife? Straighten me out when I need it, fill up my life with your sweetness and common sense, work by my side, and have our babies?''

Corrie's eyes were swimming with tears and her heart was about to burst with joy and love and the most incredible sense of peace and rightness. And a deep, deep knowledge that she belonged with this man.

''I will,'' she got out, then kissed him, eventually feeling the first strong tendrils of true frustration because just kissing Nick suddenly wasn't enough. It was Nick who ended the kiss, which sharpened that feeling of frustration.

''I reckon we ought to put on the ring before we lose it,'' he said gruffly, and Corrie drew back to watch as he singled out her ring finger and slipped the ring into place. Then his dark gaze lifted to hers and she had the most incredible sense that this decision to marry hadn't come too soon, that it would never be a mistake.

It was in those rapid pulse beats of time as she stared into Nick's dark eyes that Corrie could almost see images of what was ahead in the years to come, the joys and the pleasures as well as the normal adjustments and routine difficulties of two people making a life together, creating something far bigger and more important than only themselves. And though love surrounded those still indistinct imaginings, commitment and devotion would be the bedrock.

''I love you, Nick,'' she whispered and Nick whispered back, "I love you, lady. You'll never regret this, I promise."

Their lips drifted back together again, but the sound of a pickup engine, followed by a rude, *so* rude series of blaring honks drew them apart as Shane's pickup roared around to the back of the house and pulled in beside Nick's. Shane left the engine running and put down the driver's side window to stick his head out and yell.

"Is that a diamond on that girl's finger, or are you and I gonna raise some dust?"

Nick chuckled and lifted Corrie's left hand. "How's this?"

Shane's smile went huge then as he called back, "You don't deserve her, but congratulations, big brother! And Corrie? If that cowboy don't treat you right, you just let me know!"

"Go find a wife!" Nick yelled back.

Corrie gave a little wave and Shane touched his hat brim to acknowledge it, then backed the truck to turn before he headed around the house, leaning on the horn most of the way down the drive to the highway.

# Harlequin Romance®

*Contract Brides*

**From paper marriage...to wedded bliss?**

## A wedding dilemma:

What should a sexy, successful bachelor do if he's too busy making millions to find a wife? Or if he finds the perfect woman, and just has to strike a bridal bargain...?

## The perfect proposal:

The solution? For better, for worse, these grooms in a hurry have decided to sign, seal and deliver the ultimate marriage contract...to buy a bride!

### Coming Soon to

### HARLEQUIN® *Romance*®

featuring the favorite miniseries Contract Brides:

**THE LAST-MINUTE MARRIAGE**
by Marion Lennox, #3832
on sale February 2005

**A WIFE ON PAPER**
by award-winning author Liz Fielding, #3837
on sale March 2005

**VACANCY: WIFE OF CONVENIENCE**
by Jessica Steele, #3839
on sale April 2005

*Available wherever Harlequin books are sold.*

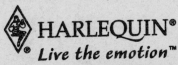

# HARLEQUIN®
## *Live the emotion™*

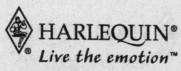

# *Harlequin Romance*®

Every month, sample the fresh new talent in
Harlequin Romance®!
For sparkling, emotional, feel-good romance, try:

January 2005
## Marriage Make-Over, #3830
by *Ally Blake*

February 2005
## Hired by Mr. Right, #3834
by *Nicola Marsh*

March 2005
## For Our Children's Sake, #3838
by *Natasha Oakley*

April 2005
## The Bridal Bet, #3842
by *Trish Wylie*

*The shining new stars of tomorrow!*

Available wherever Harlequin books are sold.

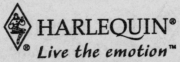

**HARLEQUIN**®
® *Live the emotion*™

**www.eHarlequin.com**　　　HRNTA1204

If you enjoyed what you just read,
then we've got an offer you can't resist!

# Take 2 bestselling love stories FREE!

# Plus get a FREE surprise gift!

Do you like stories that get up *close and personal*?
Do you long to be loved *truly, madly, deeply...*?

If you're looking for emotionally intense, tantalizingly
tender love stories, stop searching and start reading

# *Harlequin Romance*®

You'll find authors who'll leave you breathless, including:

## *Liz Fielding*
Winner of the 2001 RITA Award for
Best Traditional Romance
(*The Best Man and the Bridesmaid*)

## *Day Leclaire*
*USA Today* bestselling author

## *Leigh Michaels*
Bestselling author with 30 million
copies of her books sold worldwide

## *Renee Roszel*
*USA Today* bestselling author

## *Margaret Way*
Australian star with 60 novels to her credit

## *Sophie Weston*
A fresh British voice and a hot talent!

*Don't miss their latest novels, coming soon!*

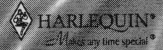

**HARLEQUIN**®
*Makes any time special*®